The Trees Swallow People

Conor Matthews

Published by Conor Matthews, 2024.

This is a work of fiction. Similarities to real people, places, or events are entirely coincidental.

THE TREES SWALLOW PEOPLE

First edition. January 23, 2024.

Copyright © 2024 Conor Matthews.

ISBN: 979-8224738717

Written by Conor Matthews.

To Those We've Lost.

I.

In a public park there are trees that have never harmed anyone, lining the path from the entrance, shaping the jogs and evening strolls people take, in places parted enough for desires lines to form. But then there are the other trees.

The trees are separated from the rest of the park by an old wall, slapped together in the last century by apprentice masons; a ring of jagged grey the path through the park goes around. There is no reason to ever be in this paddock of seemingly innocuous trees.

During a nightly walk with my dog, Diva, as she happily panted, I aimlessly turned to the patch of heavy woodland behind the old wall, glancing inattentively to the moonlit highlights on the bare branches and the few clinging leaves, following the contrasted shadows to the depths of the trunks, landing upon a face.

It took a second to realise what I was looking at. Wanting to be sure, I planted my eyes upon the shapes of soft light and etched shadows. It was the staring eyes that confirmed my surprise as they blinked back at me. Realising it was indeed a person, I submitted to the glare and turned my gaze away, hoping the man would assume I meant no offence.

As we walked, Diva oblivious to the scene, I slowly recalled what I had seen, as though still checking with myself. They appeared to be in their thirties, going by the young puff of brown hair and plump yet worn face. His hands were placed on the wall; a build taller than it but on the shorter side, maybe five-six. Was it a white hoody he was wearing? A fleece? A jacket?

I was doing laps with Diva around a football pitch next to the trees. I decided, as I tuned a corner around goal posts, I'd take a look back. From the slow movement of his head, I saw that he was following my progress across the width of the pitch. I looked away again, this time feeling the tension. There was a story weeks ago of a sex offender sleeping rough in the area. What are the chances, I thought, I had just stumbled upon the very man the rumours were about? Was I to be a tabloid headline?

As I rounded the next set of goal posts, I was parallel with the trees, which span the entire length of the field, easily a couple dozen yards. If I continued on my usual route, I'd be passing the trees and the face once again in two more turns. I turned my head, half expecting a reason to cut my walk short tonight and run home. Instead, the man was gone. I strained to make sure I was looking at the same spot as before. The night was too clear to be mistaken. I scanned the pitch, thinking perhaps he hopped over the wall. I watched the path circling the enclosed woodland. Still, nothing. I continued my walk, coming across only one more oddity that night.

After some time, I decided we were done for the night and made our way across the field and back to the path to the entrance. I gave a farewell glance to the trees, a kaleidoscope of shattered shapes amongst branches and twigs, splitting the moonlight, before returning my view ahead of me in time to see her.

A woman was stepping onto the pitch. She wasn't a jogger and was by herself, yet I paid her little attention at first, since there was a distance between our trajectories. I continued on before I recalled the story about the sex offender. I stopped and looked behind me, debating if I should continue my laps a little longer to ensure I was nearby should she call for help. I spotted the woman already hoisting herself over the wall before vanishing behind it.

I stared, bemused yet unsure of what just happened. Her stride as she passed me suggested she was going somewhere. Who would be in a hurry to jump over a wall? I imagined if you went through the woodland you'd come out the other side. But why not take the path? It was dark, the ground would be littered and uneven. I watch the wall for a few minutes, wondering if she would reappear. Was she meeting the man? Could this be a sexual thing; exhibitionism? It would explain the man, peeking out, expecting someone and watching me, hoping I'd leave. Or maybe hoping I'd stay.

At the time I left, believing I was intruding. It's childishly simple, looking back on it now. From that night on, the trees proved themselves to be anything but simple.

II.

Over the weeks, two things continued to catch my attention. First, there was a sudden increase in the number of people going missing. Upon first impressions, one would say they had little in common. For instance, one was Michelle O'Reilly, a grandmother who emigrated and returned at least twice, known locally as a music teacher who muttered swears whenever she had a particularly untalented student, reported missing by her adult daughter. Another was Anthony Winkleman, a newly married husband from the states, working in the docklands as an engagement engineer; essentially, his job was to make social media users into social media abusers.

The disappearances, at first, seemed few and far between. Rumours of strangers skulking the village circulated, taking an unnerving turn as people started recognising them as reported missing themselves on the news. Stranger still, they weren't from the village. When you count for gossip in the village shared in pubs and hairdressers with the official reports across the country, you easily realise people were going missing daily.

Secondly, it didn't take long for gardaí to be seen patrolling more often than usual. The only real times you'd see them outside of the local station were to chase kids with fireworks on Halloween or the odd fight after a few drinks and poorly chosen words. People walking alone were regularly stopped and questioned; where are you from, are you local, how's the home life? The expression "a guard wouldn't ask me that" quickly lost all meaning.

The news reported on "redoubling efforts" and "locations of interest" announced by the Garda Commissioner. I imagine the hope was conservative admission that something was happening, but being handled, was an alternative to remaining silent and fuelling speculation. Perhaps if they were still here today, the Commissioner would reconsider their strategy, given how things panned out.

From news reports, I learned the woman I had spotted crossing the field and entering the woods that night was Ciara Donaldson, an emergency services operator from Belfast, last seen by her roommate. They, according to a post made by the roommate, were talking over breakfast when, abruptly, Ciara said she needed to leave. Assuming Ciara was late for work, she thought nothing of it until she hadn't returned that evening nor by the following morning, not responding to calls or texts. I hadn't reported my sighting, despite being sure it was her now, until I saw the next person to enter the woods.

I was walking with Diva. While I had avoided the pitch and the woods for a few days, spooked by that night, I decided it was long enough to return and chalk the experience to a funny yet strange encounter. Maybe my assertion was right, I thought; maybe they were dogging. I'd be lying if I said a part of me returning wasn't in the hope of seeing a fleeting glimpse of something. I watched the horizon of trees come into view as I turned off the path and approached them, my ears and eyes searching for signs of life amongst the withering, bare branches and the almost scaly trunks, coarse and aged. The trees, with their promise of forbidden voyeurism, didn't hold my attention for long.

As we walked parallel to the wall, ignoring the decaying deciduous leaves cast aside and lying on the sloping trench that met the wall, focused on the top plate, debating if I could lift myself up enough to look within, it was Diva stopping that attracted my attention. It wasn't like her to suddenly stop. I looked down at her and followed her line of sight just in time to see another woman, this time much younger, making her way to the wall.

Her hair hung in one sheet, so dark it threatened to swallow the moonlight highlighting her. Petite yet stretched, taller than me for sure. This was Emma McNair. The only reason I knew this was I had seen reports of her disappearance before that night. She was from Sligo, barely eighteen, and I knew, from the blotchy faced sobs of her mother appealing for her return on the news, she was deeply missed.

Until I announced myself, I might as well have been invisible. She was less than four feet in front of me as she crossed my path, making no effort to avoid nor waiting for me to pass. She was determined to finish what she had started. I had joined Diva in halting, so shocked to see her, feeling as though I had just watched a fictional character enter my world, that I nearly allowed her to enter the woods without speaking. I just shouted. Not in anger, but still audible, unable to decide between "hey" and "oy", splitting the difference in the end. The effect was the same. She slowed down, stopped, looked over her shoulder, and into my soul.

Do you know that feeling when you see past someone's defences for a second? When you see the sorrow behind the hate, the fear behind the insults, the loneliness behind the bitterness? I shared this moment with Emma. I saw, for one fleeting nanosecond, an innocent soul pleading to be stopped, to be rescued from a horrible part of itself that wants to die. Like a flickering match, that soul was snuffed out, pulled back into the depths of those black, hungry pupils. The eyes, though looking straight at me, became unfocused and inanimate; the eyes of a mind eating itself.

Without a word, she turned back to the wall, approached, and climbed over it, feeding whatever laid within. I didn't investigate. I stood there for some time, along with Diva, frozen in the guilt of knowing even if I tried stopping her, it would prove useless compared to whatever was dragging her from her home, as it had done with the others, as it would do with all of us, except those unlucky enough to be left as silenced witnesses.

III.

Reporting at the Garda station proved depressingly tedious. I went, expecting to be met with derision and light mockery or perhaps aggression for wasting their time. It proved to be neither, but still a regretful experience for two officers.

I made sure Diva had enough food and water before I left. I couldn't leave the back door open for her, so I decided to accept whatever mess I would find when I returned. Already I wasn't hopeful for a brisk in-out job. I walked down the Rye hill, through Squirrel Wood, and turned at the traffic junction for the station. I pushed my weight against the heavy glass and metal doors, entering a drab interior where the light was doing a lot of the heavy lifting.

I stood in front of a reception desk behind a window. I expected a buzzer of some kind but decided to tap the glass since I could hear movement behind a divider on the other side. The noise momentarily stopped before resuming. I tried craning my head to see around the divider before knocking again. I got back a shout to wait. So I did. What I was waiting for came around to the desk minutes later; a stout, slim man, stretched out by dripping wrinkles on his face, most likely early fifties. He asked the first of many questions that day; what? I said I was a concerned citizen, I've noticed strange happenings in the woods, and I believe it's connected to the disappearances.

His pale, tired eyes stayed on me all throughout the silence. Whether bored or stunned, I'll never know. He simply got up, vanished behind the divider again, and reappeared by a secured door to the side. I was brought inside to a room to give my statement. He performed his vanishing act once again, but I wasn't alone for long as in entered a detective Murphy and a detective McGrath. They sat in front of me, began recording, introduced themselves, and began. I say began because it seemed as though they had been raring to go for some time, like hungry spiders pouncing on flies snagged in their web.

Who are you? Where are you from? What's your history? Ever been arrested? Who are your family? They started off normal enough, if a little invasive, but soon became stranger. How did you see them? What woods? Why tell us? Are you involved in a group? Are there others like you? Why are people going missing? Why are they doing this? This last one surprised me, as though I had something to do with this. Maybe, I entertained, I was the first lead they had, and thus the closest thing to an authority on the matter they had. If that was the case, my good will in coming was being worn.

No matter how often I answered, in however many ways there are to phrase a response, they went on the same questions, again and again. Even the tone shifted. The formal, bored official sounding questions gave way to rolled eyes, exhausted huffs, and glances of annoyance to each other. I was feeling impatient myself, tempted to ask may I leave when, whether through boredom or frustration, I was asked if I was willing to show them the woods.

We took the normal route myself and Diva would come; straight ahead, turn right, left by the old monastery, right at the car park, and through the gap in between the trees. I was able to strike up a friendly conversation with Murphy about Diva. He had a yorkie as well. McGrath stayed quiet, watching us. Maybe they were playing me; good cop, bad cop.

I pointed the woods out as they came into view. Even though a threatening wind stroked the blades of grass on the pitch, it had no effect on the spindly trees in the distance. We made our way to them, but I knew myself I didn't want to go the full way after what happened to that girl. I stopped half-way, expecting them to continue on without me, but McGrath gave an order to move. I knew there that I was a person of interest through no fault other than I was the only lead they had. Shocked initially, I allowed myself to be carried away by the order.

We came to the edge of the field, just at the bevel into the trench that met the paddock wall. Both Murphy and McGrath surveyed the trees, wondering aloud if they could close off the park. I thought the same as McGrath; she shot the idea down. The park had multiple entry points and stretched to Lucan, spanning over Kildare and Dublin. Murphy was just about to respond when it happened.

Flickers in our peripherals, along with the sudden swell of rustling, dragged our attention from the trees, turning in time to see them whip past us. A stampede of people sprinting across the field and narrowly missing us, like white water surging around rocks. It happened so quickly, I only caught glimpses of their blurred features. Men, women, young, old, White, Black, Asian, slim, well fed. They all formed a tidal wave of rushing bodies in the hundreds. The quiet mid-week park had been transformed into a gushing path of souls. Murphy was like me, shielding himself behind his arms, making himself as small as possible. McGrath, attempting to stop someone, had lunged to grab an arm, only to be knocked over, curling up into a ball on the ground as they leapt over her. As with the others before them, the sea of people vanished over the wall, gone forever.

It ended as abruptly as it began. No stragglers. The shushing absence fell upon the field, awing the three of us. It took a moment for the breeze to return. I faced Murphy and McGrath as they composed themselves. McGrath just got up and raced for the woods herself. Had she not called to Murphy for them to follow the horde, I would have believed she too had fallen prey to whatever madness was seeping into our helpless minds. Up and over they went, and that was it. No thud upon landing. No slap of rushing feet upon damp leaves. No heavy breath. They were gone, like the others.

I waited, straining to hear something. Even as the tinnitus from the stampede continued to ring in my skull, I was sure I was not deaf, as I still heard the white noise of distant cars along the motorway, muffled screams of joy from the playground further into the park, and the slowly swelling gust. I heard nothing from within the woods. An hour or so had elapsed. At some point, the station would wonder why the detectives hadn't returned. I reasoned I should return to the station, using the walk to figure out the best way to explain what had happened without sounding crazy. But first, I thought, I should go home and check Diva has enough food and water. I knew, even then, I would be gone for some time.

IV.

After a few days, they had the pitch taped off. A local club wasn't impressed. There were other pitches, but GAA lads aren't known for their sense of rationality. Bitterly, they relinquished. The irony of trying to keep people away from the trees was it only led to more interest in them. People approached the tape, either noticing it in surprise or clearly searching for it, stopping and pointing. Usually, the latter came in groups, setting out together to investigate.

The Gardaí marching along the tape were often called over and asked what was happening, simply replying it was part on an ongoing investigation. However, the few times someone crossed the tape, approaching a Garda they hadn't managed to attract, were met by barked orders to get behind the tape. Most would rush back, but one gentleman was particularly stubborn. It's strange the way people speak to one another with such authoritative disgust, as though a minor inconvenience is a great outrage. For this fellow, his face shoved into the muck and his wrists cuffed was all he got.

Further down the pitch by the paddock were more officers and people, differing depending on the day. First, they were just other guards, but from the chatter of those I passed in the park, gawking from the tape, they were guards from other counties. An educated guess made the rounds that they were looking for those who had gone missing. Later in the week, people in hazmat suits were scanning around the paddock. An argument sparked between the guards and the hazmat people. They were too far away to hear, but given the pair in suits entering the woods, never to be seen again, I can imagine they were warned about what happened to McGrath and Murphy.

As of late, more technical, scientific looking researchers joined the effort. Obviously they weren't in lab coats, but their large erected tents, the fact they were seen collecting soil samples around the wall, and the floodlights directed into the trees hinted at how seriously they were taking this. When brute force fails, I suppose.

Upon one of our walks, as Diva was taking her time to urinate, one of the many usuals that lined the tape daily I overheard asking had they found the drone yet. From what I gathered, earlier the researchers tried flying a drone over the trees to get a safe look inside. As I looked over, I could just make out one of the researchers still holding onto a large control panel, growing ever frustrated as it proved unresponsive, erratically shaking it. I took it the drone was lost amongst the trees too.

It wasn't only researchers the trees attracted. The theories and gossip, spanning from aliens to Satanists, had brought more and more people to the edge of the tape. The locals soon struggled to get past those from across the country and even Europe. English families in camper vans and Dutch cyclists rerouted to see for themselves the source of the tales that had reached their ears. A French couple who had been staying in Dublin wielded their broken English and worn dictionaries as best as they could to make the trek from Connolly to Confey, asking passer-bys where are "les arbres".

Despite the novelty of these strange events, the allure of the trees soon came over the visitors. One girl, a sixteen year old daughter of a travelling family from Kent, documenting their trip on their YouTube channel, ducked under the tape and bolted across the field. There was no shortage of people to catch her between her father, brother, and the guards, but still she managed to gain a good deal of distance as she wriggled, punched, and clawed, digging at the saturated muck, staining and chipping her fingernails. Despite the family pleads, she continued her manic quest for the trees, screaming incoherently, like an animal fighting to escape a trap. Her cries could be heard even as she was forced into the back of a squad car, brought to the station for questioning.

Though there were more like her, overcome by the desire to be amongst the branches, there were those who crossed the divide for other reasons. There have always been those who are incapable of accepting the world as a place that doesn't make sense. Those people soon joined the gawkers, yet what made them unique was the entitlement, the demand that this all stop, as though that's how it works. They'd loudly question the investigation, asking why aren't they going in or why are they just standing around, only to give their own answers, suggesting this was all a hoax or that the government was just trying to scare them. If only.

The level of idiocy quickly rose as these free thinkers from message boards attempted to storm past the guards and researchers, throwing punches and spitting swears as they were tossed into the back of a van. A few nights of this, with one managing to get over the wall, screaming for those missing to come out, as though they were hiding their giggling behind the trees for fun, proved to be too much. The pathway around the pitch was taped off further. Between the monastery, the playground, and the Lucan end of the park was completely off limits now. With that, many tourists stopped showing up. Outside wild speculation online, even the fearful dropped their attempts to uncover the mystery. A brief sense of normality seemed to have returned. And then I saw him.

Diva needed her walk that evening. Though the park was now sectioned off for the most part, we were still able to walk circuits. I decided a few laps around the grassy fields just as you enter would be enough. Coming up on our third lap, I could just make him out in the clear night, enough moonlight to highlight his silhouette. I found it strange right away that he was on his knees, holding up his hands, his palms facing him, mumbling something with his lips barely moving. At first I thought he was hurt, then senile, then it occurred to me he could be praying.

As I got closer, I could see he was kneeling, but still upright. His hands quivered, as if he was straining to keep them up for some time. His eyes were open and looking up into the sky at nothing in particular. I kept pace but watched him, turning at the end of the path like the previous two times. I figured I'd leave him to it, pulling out my phone to check if there was a feast day I wasn't aware of. The lap would take another eight minutes before I was back where I spotted him. By that point, he was gone. To where, I didn't know. I still don't to this day. What I do know, and what we would all learn, was that he called himself Shepard. And Shepard was praying that night. Praying to the trees.

V.

It was one of the Tuesdays when I would go to the post office down the village when I saw Shepard again. He was standing atop a raised brim of a monument on Main Street, tucked away between a taxi rank, car park, and corner shop, opposite the road, a credit union, and a pub, yet that didn't stop him from preaching, as he called it. I could hear him raving from down the street, first as incoherent calls, then becoming clearer in its lunacy as I got closer.

Once I finally spotted him, wildly looking for anyone passing by to proselytise to, I recognised him as the man praying in the park. In the daylight I could finally see Shepard has a youthful face, yet his hair had a band of grey around his head beneath his brunette crown. His angular, long face was peppered by day old stubble. His long winter coat, slacks, and leather slip-ons gave the impression he had a sense of style. I thought he was rather handsome, but then I heard what he was saying.

Come! Family of God; the Creator has blessed this nation, this community, with a miracle! Fear not, as the angels cry; what we have comes from him! God has given what is meant for us! What is intended! God has blessed us! God has blessed the trees! The trees are for us!

There was more, but I just continued on. Luckily I didn't catch Shepard's eye. It didn't seem like anyone did, though the odd few people walking the street, entering the credit union, the shop, or the pub did stare, with only two stopping for a moment before scoffing. There were jeers but they fell silent once they realised Shepard wasn't stopping. Nothing was interrupting his tirade into the air. He was clearly unhinged. I just did what I had to and returned up the hill.

I heard during the week that he was by the monument daily since then, from noon until three, calling out at the top of his lungs. The guards couldn't stop him other than give a verbal warning; it was a public space, he wasn't blocking the path, he wasn't doing it at night.

When I went down the next Tuesday, I saw he was joined by someone. A squat woman with a tangle of greying hair, searching, from the foot of the monument in Shepard's shadow, for anyone to give one of the pamphlets she clutched to her chest. As I made my way to the post office, I overheard someone passing her saying where she can put her pamphlet. Shepard was still at it.

All is an instrument in God's orchestra, to be conducted by his divinity! Just as the prophets fulfilled his glory, so too have miracles! The hungry fed from one basket! Seas parted for the exodus! Just as God acted through Muhammad, through Moses, through Abraham, so too he acts through the trees! The trees are an act of God!

You can laugh at madmen, but you can't be bored by them. Even though the overall mood was one of confused bemusement and mockery, I couldn't help but notice people were slowing down more, lingering a little longer to watch, unintentionally hearing more of what he had to say. Even in the post office, where you could just make out his howling, people in line were paying attention, to the point I had to tell the person ahead of me they were next to be served. Even the post clerks were distracted, pausing, tilting their heads to absorb more of the maddening rhetoric.

As I left, I noticed someone else had stopped completely before Shepard, gazing up at him with mystified eyes of awe. I wasn't surprised, though disappointed, when I found this same person had joined Shepard and the other woman the following week. What did surprise me was the sudden shift in his preaching.

The Lord in Heaven came down to save the world from sin as a man! The Lord appeared to Moses to save the chosen people, as a bush! And now he has come to us as the trees! Yes, God is the trees! The trees are God! Rejoice! He is here! He calls us! He has returned!

I had to weave around people frozen on the street watching. The opened windows of the town houses were perches for those who wished to listen from their homes. Even businesses were abandoned, the employees standing outside, equally enraptured. When I noticed the post office clerks were also outside, I thought I should leave, as the atmosphere was uncomfortable.

Gone were the derisive snorts, smirking shakes of the head, and the apathetic, rolled eyes. The patient watching, the anticipating standing, the feeling something was going to happen took their place. And those pamphlets were no longer hanging out longingly for a passive hand to politely take them. The stack was being circulated, practically snatched at amongst the crowd. In shock, I took the stack and only had a second or so to take in the cover before Sean Fergus, a dopey lad I went to school with, now moderate publican, yanked the stack from me, impatient to add to the five or so he was already holding. In that second, it made an impression on me.

Learn the truth with Shepard! Felling lost? Scared? Unsure? Fear not, the angels proclaim! The truth is yours to follow!

In between these words was a vector graphic of the tree of life. Whether this was intentional to allude to the trees or just a convenient way to tie Shepard back to something larger than himself, I don't know. I went to leave.

YOU!

Can you imagine what silence magnified sounds like? It is not quiet. It is the sound of hundreds of feet shuffling, clothes ruffling, the swish of turning heads all at the same time. I knew instantly, before I had even turned to face those deranged eyes, that authoritative stretched out finger, the towering stance even at a distance, that Shepard was talking to me directly.

I met everyone else's eyes, filled with distant intrigue one would give a fascinating animal in an enclosure, before I finally landed on him. I could feel my face grow hot with the mounting tension. I suddenly became aware of how hard the sun was working to penetrate the overcast sky and how strong whatever I stepped in smelled. My attention readjusted back onto Shepard, as though he willed my senses against me. And then he spoke. No yell, no shout, no command. He spoke like we were discussing something privately and not surrounded by a street full of people.

The will of God is not to be tested... The boy leaves his flock to find the stray not because it is more valuable, but because it is his... you are called... do not wane God's patience.

Silence.

I tried willing my legs to move, to take me home, to allow me to vomit my nerves up in privacy, but they refused. The church bell a little further down the street rang three. Shepard jumped down, reminding me that it was his elevation that made him look so tall; he was on the shorter side of average, about five six. And he left. It's almost funny looking at it now. He just left. I comforted myself later that night, after I felt bitter and empty, with the image of Shepard entering one of the apartments by Louisa Bridge Station, kicking off his boots in favour of pink fluffy slippers and a microwaved lasagna in bed, watching Ru Paul's Drag Race.

The others began to leave. Some still stared at me for a moment longer. Others blinked rapidly and shook themselves awake, as though coming out of a trance. Eventually, my legs listened to my internal pleading, carrying me home as my focus was drowned in a cascading sea of rumination. What just happened? What did he mean? The trees, the disappearances, the wannabe Alan Watts impersonator; when would all this madness end?

The answer to that last one, I could never imagine, would involve me hauling Shepard's limp and beaten body over my head and tossing him into the pit of those damn ravenous trees.

VI.

The fog wasn't unusual for the time of year. A damp but clear Friday night was perfect for a foggy Saturday. Letting Diva out for a piddle, I could see the neighbouring houses behind a frosted drapery of mist; doll houses under lace. I brought my coffee to the living room and shifted the blinds to barely see further than the driveway. If I had a car, I'd imagine I would only be able to make out the steering wheel in the driver's seat. Drinking my already cooling cup, I reminded myself to close the backdoor, when I heard Diva call me.

Like a beaten down husband, I shuffled off to find Diva in the kitchen, a stern look of impatience on her as though expecting an explanation as to why her bowl had yet to be replenished. I was struck with realisation; I was meant to buy dog food yesterday. Though Diva would have been happy with the chicken in the fridge, she was ageing, despite her spry personality, and I wanted to make sure she was getting the right nutrients. I resigned myself to get fully dressed and brave the mist to get a sack of nuggets. I at least allowed myself the luxury of enjoying my coffee, to Diva's impatience.

Getting to the shop wasn't a problem, not until I would get to the traffic lights, where I'd have to be extra careful; I don't doubt some eejits would be trying to find their way in this fog. As I made my way from the house, taking the path between patches of grass, approaching the "granny flats", the fog became thicker, transitioning from a wispy sea of vapour to a swallowing grey void so dense I had to wipe the droplets from my face to convince myself I wasn't drowning. I carefully planted myself with each step, a rigid half stumble, afraid to bump into a wall or lamp post, with my searching hands outstretched in front of me.

Continuing, my squinting eyes soon became strained, to the point where I depended heavily on my neglected hearing. Aside from the scraping of rubber soles against the coarse pavement and my anxious breath, I couldn't hear anything. The usual, distant tinnitus of cars skirting down the motorway a few miles to what I guessed was my left, and the atonal caw of birds waiting to descend upon abandoned scraps in back gardens were suspiciously absent.

Even my own footsteps were deaf to me, though I could make out dampen squelches of wet grass on waterlogged soil. I must have been at the patch of grass after the granny flats and before the road, I thought incorrectly. There was no way to tell at the time. I couldn't see beneath my chest. My arms, still held out, might as well be submerged in the murky depths of a bog; they were just as wet and cold as that would have been.

I continued on, stumbling on uneven divots every couple of minutes. That was the strange part. Well, stranger. I should have met the road I needed to cross within seconds of crossing the patch, or at least the hedges that frame the narrow opening leading to it. But minutes, not seconds, had passed. I didn't want to stop, reasoning I'd find something I recognised to get my bearings. Eventually, I did... The trees. The paddock. Those damn trees!

I stood there, open mouthed, looking up at them, frozen in place by the immeasurable surreality of it all. It hadn't dawned on me at the time, but the fog had cleared enough to see the trees and the wall, yet was as dense as ever anywhere else around me, like a dark room penetrated by a shaft of light from a beckoning doorway. I wasn't really shocked, nor terror-struck, but rather caught, like I had stumbled upon something I wasn't meant to see. Not only was the park in the complete opposite direction as the road and the shop, there were at least four or five estates I would have had to pass to get here; I should have come across a house or a ditch somewhere, even if I had lost my sense of direction.

Unnerved, I turned around and began to walk away, aiming for the path to make my way out of the park. But I never found the path. The wet squelches beneath me never left, like I was being tracked by a squirming tangle of slapping tentacles. At one point, to my right, I could hear the surging shush of a car, turning in time to just make out the cone of lighter shades of misty grey, its stretching reach fading into the innards of the fog. I started to make my way towards it, believing I would eventually find a road to follow. I could see, in between the shooting glances I directed to my feetless legs every time I nearly lost my balance, something forming ahead of me, first as a welcoming strip on the horizon, maybe the side of a housing estate I thought, then as a horrific, sinking revelation I childishly wished I could deny, to preserve what little faith I had in a rational world. I had returned to the trees.

I searched around me, forgetting for a second about the obscuring fog, thinking, wishing I might find someone laughing, so I may be relieved to find this had all been an amazingly pulled joke at my expense. I would have happily allowed myself to be paraded as a fool, a simpering masochist, if it meant I wasn't losing my mind. My desperate glances were cut short as I was thrown to the ground, pressed into the mud by a weight I kicked off me in fright, shooting up from my muddy impression I left, finding I was now standing over a man.

He wasn't much younger than me, though clearly not in his thirties yet. The thick mist parted enough for us to see each other, though it was still like we were divided by a curtain of sheer silk. He was tall, slim, with a tuft on his crown with the sides shaven; not bad looking. The shock on his long face told me long before his rambling outburst that he, too, was lost.

It must have been comical to see someone my height trying to calm down someone so tall as he got to his feet and began speaking without pause or inhalation. Once I succeeded, he managed to make way more sense. He said he was just walking to his mother's, who was a few doors down on his street, when he lost his way in the fog, coming to the trees. He's been trying to make his way home for the last two hours. He tried phoning for help, but had no signal nor connection. It only dawned on me there I hadn't even thought of doing that. Every time he tried leaving, he kept coming back to the trees.

He was reluctant when I suggested we try leaving together, almost fearful of me, as though I had something to do with all of this. When I told him, in agitation, I was leaving with or without him, he finally came around. From how he told it, I must have been the first person he's seen in two hours. From how he clung to my arm as we started walking, he was determined not to go another two hours without a reassuring stranger.

We went right, following the wall, walking parallel to it. The fog was thinnest here, so at least we could see a few feet around us. We should have reached the end of the pitch, meeting a fence encircling the dog park, within five minutes. We should have, but never did. The wall just continued to stretch, racing ahead of us into the void. The trees just watched, ghostly black alien figures made of starved, twisting fingers, contrasting against the distorted, desaturated fog.

Had more than the fog closed around us? Did the world morph around us to bend straight stretches into tormenting loops; a new circle of Hell just for us? We walked onwards. Ten minutes. Twenty minutes. Half an hour. An hour. I stubbornly hoped I could find something before my estranged friend's weeping sobs and whimpering calls for his mother got to me more than they already had. It didn't help that, no matter how far we went, no matter how much it felt like we were walking around in circles, neither the wall nor the trees appeared to be repeating themselves. Every couple of hundred steps there would be some unique feature that caught my eye, something ensuring us we were threading a new patch of the path.

A white teddy bear ensnared between branches. The springing, beckoning finger of a tree dangling a necklace, threatening to drop it. The fractal patterns in the wall gave way to feelings of pareidolia, as cracks, dents, and shadows contorted into faces of helpless anguish. I tried ignoring the sickening lurch in my stomach, willing me to glance again to confirm I did indeed recognise the faces. Even the grass took unfamiliar shapes, inclining and declining, bulging in swelling bumps and dipping into ruptured abscesses, growing shaggy like matted fur, and then becoming patchy and shorn. No features repeated. No face was the same. No trinket alike. The thought occurred to me that an easy escape was to just hop over the wall.

At last, a sign of progress, though strange it was, took shape ahead of us. A person, a stocky woman, was trudging ahead of us, making her way through the thick fog. I called out to her, but it was no use; she simply marched on. From the plume, more figures emerged, also heading in the same direction as us. They were to our right, our left, and even some further ahead of the stocky woman. My attempts to get anyone's attention were stifled when, from my peripheral, another person, an elderly man, came into view, dragging his legs unnaturally fast, passing us from behind. I looked back, awe struck to find more people, birthed from the mist in our wake. I only then became aware of the surrounding storm of footsteps, panting, and low moans that travelled with us. My right hand suddenly felt light and exposed. The man I had been guiding had let go of my hand, running off ahead, his face alight with renewed zest, like he was on the cusp of an oasis. And though I was uncomfortable, I couldn't stop myself, willed by shameful curiosity and overwhelming anxiety that if I stop I may be lost again in the fog. I wish I had stopped.

We came to him, arriving in the middle of another rambling sermon. Many had already arrived before us. He stood on the edge of the dipping ditch, his back facing the trees, his arms held up, cupping the air overhead with his fingers spread wide. One by one, they all fell to their knees, looking up to him, longingly, maddeningly, for his guidance, his protection. And like before, Shepard talked incoherently.

Kneel and be raised! Come and be never left! This is the omnipotence! Great horrors come for greater works, so we may learn mercy we assume! It is said "bruised hands raise men from children"! Fear not, for we are to learn! We shall grow, from the dirt to the sky! Watch now, as the trees end our lesson, reward our endurance, and ask for nothing we cannot give! Watch now, as those struck down are those who stand!

Shepard was looking directly at me when he said that final sentence. The air was drowned in silence. It took me a minute to notice that I was the only one standing. I spun on the spot, surveying the bowed heads; a veritable forest of devotees. I glossed over the man I was guiding, now with his back to me, as I returned to Shepard, who bore his piercing eyes into my corneas, carving his stern visage into my skull.

Watch our lesson end. Watch the standing fall.

The words left his mouth and struck me with enough force to startle me into a manic sprint in the opposite direction. I didn't care where I was going. I didn't care I was still lost. I didn't care if I was never found. If anything, being lost was enticing. I just wanted out. I wanted all this to stop. I wanted to not be surrounded by the most terrifying creatures on this planet; followers. I wanted to never hear the most agonisingly unnerving words that could be uttered; belief. I wanted to run as far away as I could from the most soul chilling feeling one must endure; fear. I just wanted to kill myself and live the rest of my days in peace. Suicide, contrary to the gullible, is sexy.

I collided into my front door with enough force to empty my lungs, ricocheting me onto my back, curling into myself, holding my chest, struggling to inhale enough to stop the sharp pain flowing inside my body. My surroundings cleared, despite my blurred vision. The sun, breaking through at last, seared my eyes. The world was reborn. I wasted no time to savour the surrounding beauty. I got up, search wildly for my keys, and shot inside, holding the door shut with my back. I began to shake, riding the last of the adrenaline racing through me. Diva must have been barking for some time before I finally noticed her. After all that, I hadn't even returned with the dog food.

I cooked her the chicken.

VII.

We can never go out the back ever again; there's a tree trying to get in. I don't know if it's the same for everyone else, but their trees started like mine; unobtrusively invasive. I let Diva out the back for her morning wee. The previous occupants did the back garden up, covering much of the once grassy plot in concrete, opting instead to construct flower beds, a glass house, a shed, and a little scummy pond. Despite this, there it was, a willow oak sapling sprouting out from a ruptured crack in the ground at the bottom of the back.

Both of us stood there, staring, before looking to each other, expecting an explanation. It was thin, just over a metre in height, with a sparse sprinkling of diamond leaves on drooping branches. The crack at the base was, by contrast, jagged and wide, sprawling crevices unfitting for such a small tree.

Soon the estate was alive with neighbours insisting for each other to witness what we all had in our back gardens, shocked to find none of us was unique. Mary Cullen, a woman around my age who had once felt me up in a pub after one too many pints, gifting me not with a surprise under the table but a black eye courtesy of her then boyfriend, crossed over to me. She didn't bother to ask if I had a tree like everyone else, just wishing to see mine. We were no further in the front door when more neighbours invited themselves in. Diva, who always barked whenever people so much as passed the house outside, was sent into overdrive. I tossed her into the bedroom and rushed back downstairs to the others; I don't trust that nosey Emma Murphy from three doors down to be left in my house without at least being tempted to check the drawers.

Soon, the entire village was alive with the news that every house had a tree in their back. The air was filled with shouts and calls, with hints of existential dread and just a morbid sense of excitement. Even some researchers, who were still working away in the taped off section of the park, made their way into the main village. When they weren't being aggressively questioned by locals, they could be seen talking amongst themselves at a distance from others, gesturing to houses, consulting their clipboards and strange readers they carried with them.

But eventually, as with the still ongoing trees and disappearances, people got bored. The disturbing is not synonymous with interest. Even myself and Diva just went to bed that night as easy as any other, not because we didn't understand the situation, but rather because we thought, ironically in hindsight, it just wasn't threatening. It wasn't until days later, as a sense of normality was returning, they became more of a threat.

I had opened the back door for Diva like usual, glancing at the tree, when a subtle feeling of incongruity struck me; a feeling of danger amidst the familiar. But what was it? All I could see was my garden. As Diva scurried out to do her business, I tried ignoring the annoying tickle of cold concrete beneath my bare feet, stepping out into the back, carefully taking stock of everything. I jumped as a trembling finger savoured a graze across my forearm. I laughed a little when I realised I had brushed past the tree, closer than I had realised. That was when it finally dawned on me. The tree was closer to the house. It had moved.

During the morning when the trees arrived, between showing mine to the neighbours and keeping Diva away from it, I became familiar with its exact position in the garden. It was about two metres from the back wall, in line with the back door, closer to the house than the shed but further than the glass greenhouse, and still close enough to the flower beds to cast a shadow. Now, it's five metres from the wall, in line with the greenhouse, and no longer darkening the flowers with their presence. Even the branching cracks in the concrete had moved, yet left no trail behind it. It was as if the tree just drifted closer to the house on a stream of broken reality.

I yanked Diva back as she was sniffing the trunk, retreating back inside. I knew how it would sound, but I phoned the guards to tell them what had happened. They had long since accepted what was happening in Leixlip had nothing to do with me, placing an uneasy trust in me that I really was just a helpless bystander in this bizarre life. I ignored the operator on the phone when they asked if I was "the tree guy".

An hour later, I was out the back again with Garda Sarah and Garda Grainne. Sarah was the rookie, tall and beefy, while Grainne was aged by work and smoking. Grainne took straight coffee, but I had to go looking for a lemon green tea I vaguely recalled buying when Sarah asked if I had any. There we were, all drinking, just looking at a tree. What was to be done? I said it moved. They asked was I sure. I said yes. What could they do? Arrest it? Everyone was advised not to touch their tree, but Sarah let it slip a Mr Koenig in Lough Na Mona had completely destroyed an axe, hacksaw, hedge trimmers, and a chainsaw trying to cut his tree down. Grainne barked for her to shut up, reminding her I was the Tree Guy. Before they left, they just suggested trying to record it overnight. I hadn't any security cameras, but I did have an old HD handicam when I was an aspiring Youtuber, long before I developed a sense of cringe. So long as it was plugged in and set to a lower resolution, it could be left recording all night.

So the next morning I went straight to the back, expecting to see the tree had moved. But it was in the same spot as before, as stationary as the camera on a mini-tripod on the ground. I picked it up and began scrubbing through the footage, skipping hours at a time. Aside from a brushing breeze teasing the leaves, and a creeping crescent moon in the sky, sliced by gliding clouds, there was no movement whatsoever. Disappointed, I looked up and found the tree was now less than two feet away from me.

I didn't so much as stumble back as I collapsed, overcome by the immeasurable weight of shock rooting me to the Earth, looking up to the now looming tree in nausea inducing terror like a submissive prey. My senses came hurtling back into me. I scrambled to my feet, badly scraping and scratching myself, fleeing back inside, scooping up Diva who had tried shooting outside for her morning wee. Again, I called the guards, and again Sarah and Grainne joined me later, with our cups out the back. They agreed it moved, but there was still little they could do. What did I expect? Grainne had just suggested industrial strength weed remover when we all heard the scream.

The sky filled with the ringing knell of a woman's scream, piercing at first, killing any exchange amongst those forced to hear the harrowing screech, then becoming a moaning roar, the defeated call of acceptance with panicked reluctance, continuing into a reverberating howl of pain, before finally fading into silence, leaving the entire estate standing, their ears and nightmares still ringing. I had never heard someone sound like that. I could never have imagined that was Mary Cullen.

Her neighbours on either side confirmed they heard the scream come from Mary's back. Sarah and Grainne didn't enter the house until back up arrived. We were never told what the guards found or what happened to Mary. All we saw was the house slowly, over the next couple of days, become boarded up. Her next-door neighbours said, from their upstairs windows, they could see the back was completely covered by a black tarp. And of course, the researchers were soon seen skulking outside the house only hours later. There was a rumour Grainne took early retirement and Sarah killed herself.

I was thinking about Mary days later, one morning. She was lovely. And truth be told, I didn't exactly object to her feeling me up that night in the pub. My dreamy fantasies were cut short as Diva jumped down from the bed, impatiently waiting by the door, staring at me as much as to say "well!" We made our way through the house and to the back door. Diva was excitedly panting all the way while my bare feet, still half asleep, drummed after her. I went to open the door.

I went to open the door again.

I went to open the door for a third time before I finally woke up.

The tree was right at the door. Despite its slender frame, blow after frustrated blow from the door couldn't knock it down. Through the frosted glass set in the door, I could see the scattered noise of hazy shadows pressed upon it with each thrust. Why was I so adamant on knocking this bastard down? Why was I possessed with exhausted rage? I was snapping. I was breaking beneath the weight of everything. Why was I still here? Why didn't I run? Why could I not make the world stop? Why was I only a human made of flesh and pus that'll pool in a wooden box in the dirt? Why was I still jerking my shoulder back and forth when the door stopped moving?

I froze, like a child throwing a tantrum would if they were struck. I turned slightly to my right, finding thin, coarse fingers gripping the side of the door. The branches were holding the door ajar. I looked down and saw Diva approach the parting, curious. That's when I saw a single strand of a branch slither into view, snaking up to Diva.

I lurched back, yanking the door shut. I fell, just missing Diva as she retreated back. The door shut on those ugly arboreal appendages, which squirmed like tentacles, shooting back to the outside. The blurred shadows through the glass masked the painful writhing, a maddening esoteric dance. As quickly as they began, they froze in place, pressed up against the glass.

I lay there, wondering what good was anything I could have done next. Everyone else was suffering from the same invasion. The guards do nothing. I was hardly going to ask Shepard for help. So I did what seemed right. I got up, made sure the door was locked, and from then on, Diva did her business out the front, despite the complaints from that nosey Emma three doors down.

VIII.

We're supposedly social animals, cooperative, empathetic. I'm not the most exuberant person, but I like to think I'm agreeable and can hold a conversation. I like my own company, apart from Diva's, of course. But in Dundalk, before I moved up here, I would have met up with the lads, grab a few pints, get chatting. The lads aren't in the country any more. I'm kind of glad they're not.

Needless to say, the village has gone anti-social over the last few months. I almost forgot about the trees. Coming up to night, people rush to get home. There used to be a bustle about the place on a Friday or Saturday. Main street used to be alive with girls linking arms, cackling in their soon to be broke stilettos, as they saunter pass the bouncers, and lads looking hard as they grab a table in the beer garden, pretending to know what should have happened in the football on the massive outdoor screens. I never thought I'd miss the shattered remnants of pints on the pavement. Now, from five to half six, amidst the stream of commuters from Blanch and secondary students coming in from Dublin, you can sense the paranoia. Afterwards, it's dead. The evening dog walkers are gone. The sunset gardeners watering their plants are gone. The cheeky joggers just off work making their way to the shops for a bottle or three of wine are gone. The kids cycling around the estate in infinite loops are gone. Only "They" roam the streets.

If you were to walk around yourself, you'd be forgiven for thinking I was exaggerating, as you would find people going about like normal. But look closely and you'll be unnerved by how, as you pass them, you notice them following you in the corners of their eyes. You take a turn around a corner or down an alley, only to find those who were watching you, frozen in place moments ago, have suddenly appeared ahead of you. There was talk of neighbours nodding or waving to each other in acknowledgement during the day, trying to be friendly, only to find the other person just standing there, watching them.

I'm still a little unnerved, looking back on everything, but especially by the people who stalked me. It started as I was making my way from the shops. For once, something strange began without Diva being present. I was starting to worry she was becoming a jinx. The local Supervalu was finally back in stock of some leek and cheese pasties I enjoy, so I made a trip over to stockpile on a few boxes. I also treated myself to a nice, moist blueberry muffin.

I swore under my breath at the incessant self-check out machine, barking orders in their little robotic feminine voices. I wondered, as I left, do they make them sound like women because a man's voice sounds too threatening, or was it because we're raised most by our mothers and thus are used to hearing orders at that cadence? I amused myself with the idea that some futurist they hired as a consultant for the machines was reading too much Freud at the time, which is why I didn't notice "them" at first. It wasn't unusual for people to be walking the same way from the shops; the estate across the road was large enough. I was only really aware once I casually glanced behind me, taking in no greater detail than just someone a few metres away. Once at the traffic lights, as I waited, I noticed the person behind me had stopped just short of outside my peripheral. I panned my head just enough to dart my eyes further left. I had to double take.

Standing still a few metres away, but looking directly at me, was the figure from before. With my full attention this time, I saw they were a man, in a tacky, bright blue wool jumper, with thinning short hair, staring directly at me. He had this strange expression on his face. It wasn't a smile, and he didn't sound like he was laughing, but it was as if I had caught him mid chuckle; his mouth was agape, his cheeks were plump and dimpled, and his eyes were wide and dilated. It was like something from the Uncanny Valley, uncomfortably human yet still alien. More jarring, still, was the fact he was not alone.

Behind him was another, taller man wearing a Celtic jersey with runners and tracksuit bottoms from two different brands; ironically he didn't look the exercise type. He too was staring at me with the same bizarre look. Amazingly, the dopey grin and slowly drying eyeballs were almost identical to each other, as though they were twins.

I stood there, frozen in their hypnotic gaze. It took a moment for sense to seep back into me, reminding myself to blink. I looked around, thinking I was blocking their view of someone else. No. I suddenly became aware that I was alone. This was a pretty busy road on any other day, but here I was, on a Thursday afternoon, alone with four hungry eyes lying in wait. I quickly checked for traffic before I briskly crossed the road, cutting through an opening in a row of hedges, looking over my shoulder back at the two men who were following me again, with their unnerving grins and protuberant eyes.

I tripped stepping onto and off another road, and again as I stepped onto another grass field, taking the desire line cutting through it. I could neither gain nor lose distance from the men. It's a blur, but I have a hazy recollection, less a memory and more a sense, that they were purposely matching my pace, in step with each one I took. They could easily have caught up with me, but they didn't. With the house finally in sight, I sprinted, forcing myself not to look back. The drumming sound of them sprinting too in my ears was torturous. I reached the house, got in, and held the door shut, bracing myself for a force that never came.

After I caught my breath and my heart settled, I stood up from my lunge, checking my hands, reddened and worn by the pressure they pressed against the door. They quivered with adrenaline. I looked through the frosted glass set in both the front and porch doors. I couldn't make out any misshapen shadows or distorted figures on the other side. I went into the front room, thinking I could see clearly through the window. I was right, I could see clearly. I was thrown down and anchored to the floor by the sheer fright of the two men leering in at me from the window.

Once again, I was immobilised; a prey waiting for the kill it couldn't avoid. But they just stared. Smiling, silent, staring. After what felt like forever, a sharp inhale reawakened my senses, sending me scrambling back out into the hall, doubling back to grab the door handle and pull it shut. I rang the guards, though I had to convince myself something productive would actually get done this time.

By the time they arrived, the men had vanished, and I could tell the officers weren't thrilled they had to deal with the Tree Guy again. They spoke to me with an odd detachedness, as though they were both scared and annoyed with me. I can't blame them. Between what happened with McGrath, Murphy, Emma, and Sarah, my phone calls were practically omens to them now. It didn't matter though. They just took down my statement, advised me to stay in populated areas and stay in after sundown. The dull, monotonous delivery was well rehearsed. Once they left, I practically barricaded myself in, locking everything from the front doors, the living room, the back rooms (thankfully the tree still pressing against the garden door saved some effort for me), and then the kitchen, retreating up to the bedrooms. I lived like that for days afterwards.

I tried to avoid going outside for as long as possible, but I was running a little low on food, and everything had been quiet, besides Diva's whimpers as I forced her to do her business in the house, or her yelps of restless boredom being cooped up inside. Maybe they were gone, I thought. Maybe I could take Diva out for a stroll, suss things out, then go to the shops. The thought of those leek and cheese pasties did cheer me up a little. It was a struggle to put Diva's leash on, she was that excited. I was cheered up more when an uncontrollable laugh burst out of me because Diva wasted no time planting a nice fat shit in front of the house. It was cloudy (the sky, not the dog faeces), but I didn't care much. I was feeling normal again. That was until I looked up.

She said hello. That's what startled me at first. I hadn't heard her approach, yet she was no less than a metre away from me, standing there, with her hands against her back, and that horrific, demented grin paired with that hungry leer. She repeated her greeting. It took me a second before I went to say hello back, only to be interrupted with another start; who are you?

I was confused, which she must have sensed because she repeated herself. I rebuffed her, asking who she was instead.

Who are you?

That's all she said.

Who are you?

I tried coaxing an answer out of her, saying I asked her and she was the one on my property.

Who are you?

I threatened her, acting like I would actually follow through. I thought if I got in her face, invading her space, she'd back off. She took a big step forward, just as I was about to, zooming up into my face so quickly I buckled and took a step back.

Who are you?

I gave up, pulling Diva with me, and simply walked around the woman. I looked over my shoulder, half expecting her to follow me like the two men from before, but she didn't move. She was still standing outside my house. I froze, debating if I should go back and demand she leave. I decided against it. If she was still there when I got back, I could always just phone the guards again, ensuring she didn't disappear like the men from before. Until then, I was determined to enjoy our walk.

For one wonderful hour, I forgot the world was ending. Kids were scattered throughout the estates, nowhere within sight of their houses, squealing in delight, darting around like a dispersed swarm amongst the toys and the games littering the greens and the chalk figures smiling on the footpath. The odd car sailed slowly past, drifting along a stream of tarmac and exhaust fumes. The parade of houses I pass, a gallery of properties I could never own, inspiring with their unique flourishes hidden in plain sight; welcoming fixtures and adornments in the flowerbeds, the comforting pattern in the bricked driveway shaping rudimentary shapes that now seem exotic, the still hanging Christmas lights along the roof that hark back memories of the warmth and beauty I can look forward to again and again and again. A brook etching its way from the canal, boring under roads and trees, babbling in crevices, sprinkled with fallen leaves, branches, and rocks; a welcomed treat for the heron resting its feet in the water.

We passed the park, only half interested in remembering if we were allowed back inside, but even the glimpses inside were soothing. The grass was coming up in shaggy stalks. The grounds stood peacefully alone, devoid of intrusion or worry. Lapping past the park, we made our way back home, passing cul-de-sacs and that brook again, soaking up the smells of pollen and stewing dinners for later from open kitchen windows. That didn't sound too bad to me; a nice marinade of broth in the slow cooker. Rice, peas, carrots, something like a Yangzhou or risotto. We turned the corner leading to the house.

Have you ever seen a mass of people? Not a crowd, a mass. In a crowd, people stand close together but comfortably apart. In a mass, a force squeeze people together, rubbing up against each other, body to body. In a crowd, people are autonomous and individual, all capable of looking in different directions. In a mass, like the one right outside my house, people all look in the same direction; in this case, directly at me.

I don't know what to call this feeling; La Nausea? Sartrean? Agnosthesia? Randomania? It's the feeling where you know you are looking at something you're familiar with, only to have it suddenly become alien and abstract. Who knows what a mass of people, all mad in their demented happiness, waiting for you outside your house looks like? Regardless, I knew one thing; no matter what I felt, I would have to walk past them to get home.

Each step was agonisingly laborious. Joints turning and tendons flexing felt rusty and heavy. With every step, the uncanny blurs, inhuman and indiscernible, became clearer, growing grotesque and mocking in how unwelcoming their toothy grins and starving eyes were. Even Diva, usually pulling me by the hip to get home, was now cowering, reluctantly following as I pulled the leash. I caught glimpses of neighbours peering out from windows, shielded behind smoke stained lace. Had they been waiting for me? Had they, like me, been caught off guard by the sudden gathering outside my house?

Like a passage of people, they watched me approach and enter the clearing they made that led to the front door. I had to fight the urge to stop and survey the monstrous absurdity surrounding me to fully appreciate the living walls threatened to descend upon me. I marched on, my eyes locked on the door ahead of me. Diva's leash was now so short I was nearly tripping over her as she went to rush for the door. I didn't dare look, but I knew, just from the tension and heat, all eyes were on me. I finally reached the door. I pulled out my keys, calmly placed them in the door, and entered.

Before I could finally give in and erupt in panicking gasps with the door closed, I heard a knock at the door. Staring at the ground, I slowly mustered the strength to raise my head and look through the glass set in the doors. Pressed against the front door, like the tree out the back, was the mass of people, overcasting the porch in shadow. I could see a hand rise up, pull back, and knock once more. I just stared, unaware Diva was wildly gnawing her lead to escape. Tens of blurry hands rose into the air, pulled back, and knocked. This time the house itself rang with thuds, from the door to the walls and windows. Again, they knocked, striking my home, now a prison, for a fourth time, reverberating like a kneeling bell.

I was trapped.

IX.

It had been days since we were trapped. What little light was managing to penetrate the forest of people outside my windows came in stages of intensity; soft bars in the morning, sharp beams by lunch, and an illuminating haze by dusk before quickly plunging the house into darkness. It felt like we skipped Summer with how early night came.

Tinnitus began to set in soon after that. From the banging on the house, I could feel nothing but a storm in my grey matter, a constant rumbling of rolling thunder beneath my scalp. If I concentrated, I could notice when the banging stopped and what I was hearing was my own skull reverberating. I noticed it was never the same people by the windows for long, though I never spotted the changing of the guard. This was usually when there was a brief reprieve, when the plates didn't rattle, or when Diva wasn't cowering beneath the bed. I imagined, as I savoured the sweet calm before the next imminent cascade of torment, this is how breath must feel in between waterboarding sessions. It was Hell and Heaven seconds apart.

After the first day, they cut the power mains to the house. The darkness of the night was only magnified both by the bodies shrouding the windows and the fact I didn't have so much as the microwave's LED clock for light. My phone was turned off to save energy but also because there was no point. The guards weren't responding to my calls. I could even see one every now and again standing in solidarity with the other brainless zombies. What of my neighbours during my captivity? Were they too met with apathy from the guards? Were they just glad it was me and not them? Were they among those outside? I don't blame them for not helping.

I managed to sort out food pretty well at first. I was amused initially by the surreality of having to eat a tub of ice-cream to keep it from melting since the freezer stopped working. Most things had to be thrown out once the smell started to get too much to ignore. It wasn't long afterwards that I had to resort to using the fireplace to make bland stews.

It was the night I was left with no other option than to use my hands to scoop out cold baked beans from a tin, chasing it down with the bread heels I was pretending weren't going bad when things took a drastic shift. I was just going for another scoop, sauce coating my fingers between my lips, when my tinnitus suddenly stopped, and so did the banging.

I was caught off-guard, my fingers gliding out of my mouth, disgustingly sensual, as I looked to the closed kitchen door; I didn't want Diva seeing me like this.

My breath, a sound I had forgotten, filled the silence like the washing tide filling a shore, raspy, wheezy. I strained to hear over my stupid lungs. I held my breath.

...

The crash came from the kitchen window behind me, a symphony of glass shard cymbals, trumpeting thuds, shattering violins, and a chorus of stinging night air. Diva, barking erratically upstairs, accompanied the composition as the countermelody.

I threw myself across the kitchen, stumbling, leaving the tin to splatter on the floor. I hit the fridge pretty hard, dropping to the floor, turning to grip my shoulder in agony, my legs sprawled out before me. The house finally came to life as power returned. A hallway light I forgot I hadn't turned off illuminated the intruder in a soft bounce.

He was naked, slim, tall, and pale. His hair was a nest of auburn, his eyes big enough to swallow mouthfuls, and that smile... It was the same horrible, warped, mocking smile as those things outside. I didn't even notice the knife in his hand until he raised it to his throat, already slitting it as he spoke.

You are the Witness.

I watched, in shock, as he trembled against his will but succeeded in pulling the blade across, his body becoming baptised in a waterfall of dark blood. His eyes bulged as he struggled to breathe; he must have opened his oesophagus, drowning himself. His head bounced as he dropped to his knees and fell slump on the floor, like a freshly killed livestock. That smile never faltered.

The crowd outside was gone. I never thought to check if they were gone after the messenger killed himself upon delivery of that cryptic line. The pool of blood had slowly crept outwards and had stained my feet when I decided, coming back, to phone the guards. To my surprise, they came.

I told them what had happened. We were all just so tired of this; exhausted with these nonsensical acts. The village was either going slowly mad, throwing themselves to the trees, joining Shepard's cult, or were packing up and leaving. And there was me; Tree Guy. The depressed guy with a dog. The guy who lost his partner to cancer. The guy having an affair while she was in the hospice. The guy who wasn't even there when she passed. The guy who wished he followed through and killed himself instead of chickening out.

That's me. That's Tree Guy.

They packed up the body. They told me they needed to treat the house as a crime scene. I went upstairs to pack; I'd need to spend a few nights in a hotel. This would be the first time since Michelle passed that I had slept anywhere other than in our bed. I sat on the bed, I cradled our whimpering dog, and I bawled. The sheer weight of how helpless I was in my life was only now dawning on me. I cried and kept crying even after my eyes began to sting. I drenched myself in tears and spit, hopeful I could wash away my pain. It was all too much.

The guards were nice enough to give me an hour.

X.

The invitation to meet Shepard was hidden amongst the clutter of post I had let pile up over the days. It was late August by this point. I'm only now okay. Okay-er, anyway. The village is growing quiet. Of course that's due to desertion. People have continued to vanish. It's no longer just strangers disappearing. Now it's people you know the name of; Jack the newsagent, John the barman, Colina the trad singer. The once giddy gossip of Mr. So-And-So has turned tactless. Tragedies are only fun at a distance. Besides the disappearances, people were also hitching up posts, so to speak, and leaving in droves. Many weren't even bothering to wait for the "for sale" signs to go up; houses were gutted overnight.

In my depression, I had allowed the post to gather. I don't think anyone is really in the mood to hear about the exciting new offer if they switch banks when the very same bank had to close due to non-existent employees. In a half-hearted attempt to rebuild my confidence, I made the effort of getting the post. Underneath bills, take-away menus, and people selling knives and power washers, I found it; a plain white envelope addressed "The Witness".

The Witness? It was my address. There was no stamp. This was hand delivered. I studied the envelope and its crisp, sharp corners, with a clear, pure white surface free from smudges, and the neat handwriting across its face. On the other side was a return address; "Shepard, 9959 Ryevale Lawns, Leixlip, Kildare".

My eyes stung as the air hit every millimetre I exposed in my shock. I read and reread that name over and over, refusing to admit to myself that I was correct. Shepard. Just one name. That's it. Even before I opened the unsealed flap, untucking it, I knew what this was about. Maybe that day back in the village, when he spoke to me, was his first attempt. This was his second.

To whom it concerns. *A Chara. Maidin Maith Duit Ar Maidin Seo Agus Gach Maidin*. I trust this letter finds you well, yet hope it leaves you all the better. I believe the time has come for our acquaintance to be solidified into something more developed and familiar. As such, I would be honoured and humbled if you would accept my invitation to a discussion at my current residence (see return address) on Wednesday the twenty-fourth at one o'clock in the afternoon. Lunch will be served. Should assistance be required with transport, I'll have two followers of mine escort you, otherwise I look forward to your independent arrival. With prayers, Shepard.

This may surprise you, but I wasn't unfamiliar with this kind of letter. While unemployed, I'd often receive "invitations" to attend seminars, job activation schemes, and other such bull. I almost appreciate how honest Shepard was. Just like with social protection though, I accepted I was going. What else was I going to do? Refuse? Have more psychopaths kill themselves in my house?

It's funny. This Hell, this ceaseless, formless nonsense of abject terror, it has a lot in common with the feeling of being unemployed. The lack of direction, the insurmountable size of chance and happenstance I'm expected to climb, the rumination of why; why don't you have a job, why are the trees eating people, why don't you apply for other things, why are people losing their minds, why don't you consider bar work, why am I scared to leave my house now? Awash in life, stranded in a blistering storm of howling nothingness, a cavalcade of capitalism and meaningless randomness. So what else was I going to do? I went.

Ryevale Lawns isn't far from me. It was just a case of leaving the estate and crossing the road, passing the seasonally empty school and the perpetually empty church, down the Rye hill, pass the nursing home, across a shallow river waiting to swell with the Autumn rain, and up a steep slope. This end of the village was just as bad for desertion as my side was. Houses lay hollowed like freshly picked snail shells, their occupants torn out by the crows of fear. At least one had the door just left open, revealing a glimpse through the bare home and out the back door; a cavern tempting to whistle with a lonesome breeze and ring with the echo of fading family memories. I got to the house and stood outside.

I don't know what I expected. Maybe a campsite, something like a new age group drumming and singing in tongues. But it was just a house. There was even a car outside in the driveway; a dark blue twenty-eighteen-two Skoda. I hummed to myself, bemused, before continuing up to the door. I didn't even get to ring the doorbell before Shepard opened the door. His smile, the sincere crinkle around his eyes; it was endearing, almost beautiful, how happy he was to see me. For a second, I was taken by how he was kind of handsome up close; a bit too old for me, but then again, if he wasn't a religious nut, who wouldn't fantasise about cuddling with an older man on the sofa on a rainy Saturday morning. As he spoke, my eyes drifted down to his feet.

It was foretold, and it is done! You came. I knew you would. They knew you would. This... this is the good word they have told me about. And you, you shall be the parchment which shall carry those words; the sacred vessel from which the cleansing of our sins will be birthed, a herald of our salvation. Welcome. Welcome, and thank you, Witness.

He was wearing the fucking slippers! The slippers I jokingly imagined him wearing all those months ago! That's all I could think of in that moment. I was only half listening to what Shepard was saying. In fact, he said way more than that. It's just that's all I could remember looking back now. I just couldn't believe it. It wasn't even like they were a similar pair or that they reminded me of the original pair. No. They were the exact pair I had imagined. I swore to myself in that moment, if this fucker's got lasagna in the microwave and Ru Paul streaming, I was going to lose my mind.

Enter. We have much to discuss.

His words snapped me back to the present, and I entered as he stepped aside to let me in. If it hadn't been for those slippers, I may have noticed, before stepping in, and definitely before Shepard closed and locked the door, that while the outside of the house was unassuming, the inside was a different matter altogether. It was crowded. Not so much you couldn't move around but enough where you felt like you were at a house party, though I don't know what house party features people just standing around. It was as though they were frozen in time, living mannequins that only swayed slightly due to the rhythm of their breath. In the hallway, one faced the stairs. One on the second step was looking directly at me, though I think that was more because I was standing in her eyeline. Someone in the kitchen was staring at a cabinet.

Shepard stepped forward, gauging my expression before smiling, gesturing to an open door into the front room. I followed him and once again stopped, startled to find more people. Again, few enough to move around, but enough to feel claustrophobic. They were again looking in every possible direction, unblinking, unmoving. Aside from the people, the room was bare and featureless; no sofas, no chairs, nothing on the walls

Shepard phased through the room, almost swelling his chest, as though to prove how sure he wouldn't knock into someone he was. There was a charisma about him now; a reassuring calm. Where was the screaming lunatic from down the village? What happened to the disturbing man I found gathering victims in the middle of a consuming fog? This Shepard was less Manson and more Koresh. He spun on his heels and sat crossed legged on the floor in one fluid movement. He smiled as he told me to sit.

Told, not invited.

Maybe he was hoping I wouldn't notice if he smiled, but his tone betrayed his laborious grin. It was sharp and exact. A stab of a syllable. Sit. I was stunned, reminded this man I was entertaining fantasies about was in fact a cult leader. I knew better than to pause for too long. I became aware of just how foolish I had been in coming here. In hindsight, I had let defeatism get the better of me. I sat down, less gracefully than Shepard, who watched me groan my way down. On the floor, I gave a cautionary glance to the bodies that stretched above us, like fleshy redwoods. Was that deliberate?

Shepard began, drawing my attention back to him.

So... you're the Tree Guy?

He didn't bother to wait for my response.

I understand, of course; people do like to simplify things. Especially when it comes to the order of things. Misnomers are bound to occur. Of course, no one reasonable would call you the Tree Guy.

Weird thing to be pissy about, but okay.

We, of course, know what you truly are. And what our titles are.

I didn't respond. My silence must have been inviting because he leaned in to satisfy what he must have misconstrued as anticipation on my part.

I am the Shepard. You are the Witness.

That night came flooding back to me, like the tide of blood expelling from that slit throat beneath a manic smile. It didn't help Shepard had the same look of unnerving glee.

Yes, that's right! We all have our honours, though it takes great humility to accept our own. The worm who welcomes the embrace of the bird suffers less than the lion who wishes to remain a cub. My honour is to guide the few to salvation, to rudder through the storm. Hence, I am Shepard.

First the slippers blew my mind, now I find out Shepard isn't his name! In that moment, I was just praying he wasn't going to tell me his name was something like Benedict or Terrance. He continued.

Like all those before me, I have the honour to lead the few. But all prophets need their gospels, their psalms. You. You are our Witness. That is why you were the first to see though you were blind. The trees will not harm us. Years from now, when we are all held in the sublime, we will read your words and hold you up as our apologist. And that is why I wished for you to be here today, Witness.

Slowly... the house full of people turned to face me, with stoney eyes of judgement. Maybe they were expecting me to run. Maybe they were hoping I would. I focused on Shepard.

Not yet, but soon I will invite you to join me on excursions. They'll be local. I know how you enjoy your walks with... Diva, was it? In any case, I'd like you to come and just, well, witness. The clue's in the name, I supposed.

Shepard chuckled, though his eyes never left mine, checking if I'd laugh too.

For the god above us gave us words to speak but knowledge to listen. Now, you could always refuse. Deny your place in the annals of history...

As Shepard spoke, the forest of bodies around us bent towards us, swaying in the foreboding power of his words. I tried my best to focus on him, but unlike him, I wasn't at ease with a room full of people closing in on me.

...You could say no thank you to my offer. You'd have every right to. But know this; as I said, we all have our titles. Even when we refuse one, another in more forcefully placed upon us. I'd doubt you'd like your next title any better. And I promise you, I will not extend the same pleasantries I have today should you be placed in the role of Hasatan.

I look back on it now and think it was interesting that he should use that word. It means "adversary" in Old Hebrew. It's where we get the name Satan from. On the matter of Shepard's "offer", what else could I say? The fight was beaten out of me. I just wanted to be left alone. I never wanted any of this. The next best thing I could do is just minimise my suffering. Just go along with him. So I said yes. Maybe he was right; maybe fighting has been the problem. Still, that disgustingly pleased look on his face, like he just negged me into bed, sat in the pit of my stomach, threatening me with a feeling of gurgling bile tickling my throat.

He offered me lunch (I'm nearly sure I could hear the microwave being turned on), but I said I had to go for Diva's walk. Something Shepard ended our conversation with followed me all the way home. It was so conspicuous that I immediately regretted my decision.

I wonder what role Diva will play in all this?

XI.

I felt like going for a walk. I mean, I always do, but this particular time I really felt it, like I was strongly carried against a tide of weak reluctance by something persuasive. I skipped breakfast (a lonesome cup of coffee) and would have left without Diva if it wasn't for the fact she bit into the hem of my jeans. As I put on her harness, fighting her excited squirming, I couldn't help but think how unlike me it was to forget her. Whatever had got into me it was intoxicating. I was focused completely on the walk, specifically, for whatever reason, to St. Catherine's Park.

We were only a few minutes outside when I noticed a stark difference since my meeting with Shepard. Those in the village who only weeks ago were plaguing my home, imprisoning me with gum-bleeding, teeth splitting smiles, were now passing without giving notice. I felt an ease going out now, like I was given an unspoken promise to be left alone. It was a relief.

I've often struggled with confidence and once heard it described as the ability to know you will be okay, no matter what. For me, there was always that voice that would tell me in detail how everything could go wrong, everything that was wrong with me. Now, I felt different. I felt safe.

Well... safer.

I wasn't ignorant of the still present oddity. Even with my newly stated "made man" status, I wasn't happy with how things were. I certainly wasn't going to forget about those who died, disappeared, or left. I still think about Mary. But it was nice to feel something even remotely positive. The weather was pretty fair, as I picked up the pace a little, pulling Diva along from the leash clip on my belt loop. She had to scurry and urinate at the same time to keep up. I laughed a little, entertaining the idea I was manic. It would have explained a few things. I didn't dwell on it, for the speed at which I was going once I passed the park gates took even me by surprise. Diva, her pants a snorting chortle, strained to keep her tiny paws in step with me. Even I grew worried, yanking her closer to me so she could keep up.

My feet seemed possessed, robbing me of agency. An alien drive filled my senses; get to the trees, get to the trees. My short-lived comfort in this new paradigm evaporated as I stumbled and tripped on the uneven and littered path. Coming into the latter half of September meant the still freshly fallen leaves of early autumn felt wrong as I stepped on them and the shiny chocolate bar wrappers that crinkled. I was in denial, wondering out loud, in between swears, where we were going. They (my feet, that is) took a sudden left turn, passing the dilapidated monastery, shunting myself and Diva down the path, passing the wilting flower beds; a stretching grave of brown. Leaning back and attempting to brake with my heels jolting into the ground did nothing; it was as if I was pulled by an invisible force. Poor Diva was stumbling over herself, barking in desperation. Frightened, I reeled her in quickly and pulled her up into my arms.

Another turn and, despite my attempts to stop, we're through the opening between a row of evergreens, passing the empty dog park, and we're heading for the paddock. My body is about to send me into the trees. It's those strange, alien moments that remind us how easily swept away we as frail humans can be by the sheer motion of action. Normally, it's only glimpses we catch ourselves in, forgetting why we're in a room, cheating with someone not worth a ruined relationship. Yet here I am, pulled forward by a "me" I never wanted to admit exists, a "me" that always keeps me company.

I've always been suicidal to one degree or another. I imagine it works like any other addiction; the threat of relapse will always be there. Like an alcoholic who can stay sober but always want a drink, I have to make my limbs go rigid to not jump onto train tracks. But this... I never wanted this. I never wanted the blame to be hauntingly my own. They'll blame the trees, and maybe they'll be right, but in my final seconds, I thought, it'll be a twinge of excitement, of relief, of lust that'll undercut the sheer terror coursing through me. A fetishistic gore; existential ero-guro. I wanted this. In a final act of humanity, I detached Diva from the leash. Despite her barks, her feeble attempts to pull me back, her weak, lost, lonely whimpers, I continued.

I should be dead.

But I heard something.

I stopped, dazed, as though awoken from a dream that had just incorporated the very sound that stirred me, a strange amalgamation of the illusionary and reality, casting a haze before my very eyes. Once again, I heard him call out, this time clearly.

HEY! GET OFF THE FUCKING GRASS!

I stood there, facing the trees. I was feet from the wall, about to reach the edge of the trench sloping down to it. I let the words ring out, listening. I scoffed, amused. I was saved by swearing. I turned around and found, standing by his John Deere UV, one of the park rangers, looking at me with his hands on his hips. He was a tired, sour looking man; the kind of bald scalp and slack face that made him look far older than he probably was, but not nearly as old as he was in spirit. He was the kind of person you knew from how they just stood was a joyless dick. This was Euen.

What are you doing!

I looked around, making sure it was me they were addressing.

Yeah, I'm talking to you, ya thick! You can't have your dog off the lead!

Apparently, somewhere back at the beginning of the pitch, a new sign was erected; "No dogs allowed off lead beyond this point". With the researchers, news crews, and visitors now growing bored with the trees, they had left the pitch in a state of disarray. Large patches of the pitch were torn up muck pits, carved by tire marks and water logged. In an effort to salvage things, it had been reseeded, which meant the pitches for the time being were strictly off-limits. I apologised, but that wasn't good enough.

THERE'S A SIGN! Can't you see the fucking sign!

Once again, there was that beautiful, wonderful humanity; the insistence that the world is wrong and we are right. I really can't believe it when I come across it. Even in all this mayhem, it almost brings a smile to my face to be reminded that we are delusionally pathetic, wonderfully immature, and cosmically overwhelmed by just how meaningless we are. And here was Euen, desperate to keep order. I doubt I could communicate to him what had just happened, how he had saved me from oblivion, how I had fought to stop myself. What would be the point? After all, he was growing agitated with me when I didn't respond.

Hello! Are you deaf!

I put Diva back on the leash and walked home, going straight to bed. For one night, for the first time in a long time, I slept undisturbed by conflicting wishes to end everything and a deep fear of death. I slept peacefully.

XII.

I was sleeping when the bangs echoing across the house finally stirred me. In the blissful, groggy sort of state, where you're not yet a person, still a bag of organs that occasionally moves, I just accepted someone was at my front door without feeling the need to hurry. Before all this, perhaps I would have sprang out of bed, leaping into the air and landing on the unswept wooden floor with my bare feet and unclipped toenails, the patter of slapping soles across the floor marching as I race to answer the front door, but now... now I take my time, rising with monumental effort, a slog of sluggishness. The door hammers once more, bringing back a flicker of a nightmare I endured. I take the time needed to talk myself up enough to stand and make my way to the door, Diva trotting behind me in a spritely dash. When I reach the door, however, she retreats, cowering, whimpering. I ask her what's wrong, but the only answer I get was the lowered stare at the silhouette behind the door's privacy window. Tall, squared.

I opened the door to Shepard, who was flanked by a few of his followers, including the woman who was passing out pamphlets down the village when I first came across him. His smile quickly engulfed the scowl he tried hiding as soon as the door was pulled open; perhaps he didn't expect it to be opened so soon. I'm still not okay with how handsome he is; a refined salt-and-pepper professor type. Think Pierce Brosnan now, if he had a Ra's Al Ghul kind of vibe. I'm not a bottom, but Jesus!

BLESSINGS TO YOU!

I jumped. Shepard tempered himself with a croaky cough, clearing his throat, realising he was being louder than he meant to be with me. I imagine it's a force of habit after proselytising all day. Besides the woman from before, I didn't recognise the others with him. They didn't seem familiar from the day I went to Shepard's house, so for all I know, they could have been people he picked up today. I wasn't aware if he ever left Leixlip, but it wouldn't be too difficult for people from

Maynooth or Lucan or Blanchardstown to have come across him or gone to see about the weird man who talks about trees they heard about from a friend of a friend.

Blessings to you, Witness. May we come in? I wish to ask your opinion on a matter.

I scanned over the others, unsure if I was comfortable with strangers I had yet to be introduced to entering my home. But then again, I was hardly going to suddenly bounce with joy at the same prospect if I caught their names, so I just stood aside holding the door open. Shepard was barely a foot in the door when Diva, who had been peeking out from around the kitchen door, came hurdling out towards them, barking animatedly, lifting herself up in energetic skips. Shepard merely smirked, going to say something, but it was the woman from the village who caught my attention, as she pull back her foot to kick Diva. I only realised what had happened next after I stood towering over her, her back to the wall, clutching her shoulder. I had rushed forward and tackled her, pressing her up against the wall. Unbalanced by myself and her suspended leg, she fell to the ground, landing on the shoulder I bounced off the wall. In that narrow hallway, I could feel all eyes on me. I wavered between shocked embarrassment and emboldened fury. No one hurts my dog.

I looked over to Shepard. I must have still been glaring, because he leaned back a little from fright. I'm kind of one of those deceptively strong guys; in another life maybe I could have been a gymnast. Shepard's surprise was brushed aside in place of a forced smile.

Tabitha doesn't like dogs. The others can wait outside.

A few of the followers came to lift the woman, Tabitha, apparently, who shook them off of her once she was on her feet. She gave me a snarling glare and retreated back through the front door with the others. I shouted at Diva to be quiet. She gave a few yaps and yips before grumbling and scurrying off back into the kitchen. She pissed in the back hall to show her displeasure.

Shepard sat down at the kitchen table as I prepared the coffee. I was expecting him to speak, but he politely waited over the gruelling hum and cranking of the coffee machine hard at work, and then for me to bring over the cups, milk, and sugar, and for me to take my seat across from him.

Samhain is upon us! A time of remembrance, but also of faith.

He's talking about Halloween. Samhain was the Celtic origins of it, where the end of the harvest signalled the beginning of winter and when the spirits come to visit. I didn't say anything. I waited for him to continue.

As you can imagine, the trees are linked to every fabric of this mortal world. The trees are both here and beyond. We have been showing them reverence, but I feel for this Samhain, as a sign of respect and commitment, we should do something special. Up until now the trees themselves have chosen those who join them, entering their domain. Now, however, I am called to make the choice for them. But I must admit, I do not believe I can make that decision. I hear names, calling out to me, but none feel fully right. I even thought maybe it should be me, a martyr for those yet received by the grace of the divine. Neither that struck me as accurate, either. So I come to you, Witness, the last man left but the first to know, thou blessed to be burdened with the duty of seeing and telling, what name comes to you? Who do you think that should be made whole with the trees?

THE PARK RANGER!

...

I have no idea why I said that, and as soon as I saw the smirk on Shepard's face, I wished I could have sucked back the words from the air, like extracting smoke through a vent. I wished I had been struck mute and deaf, alone in a darkness of disorientating touch.

The park ranger, you say? In Catherine's park?

Shepard watched for my reaction for a moment before looking off to the side, searching his thoughts.

What was it again? Eustace? Was it Eustace? No... Euen!

He turned back to me.

That's it, isn't it? The bald one?

I nodded, still dismayed by my response. My body seemed unconcerned with surprising me now with its sudden sense of independent autonomy. Shepard seemed satisfied.

Yes, I know the very one you're talking about. Didn't take too kind to our offerings to the trees a few weeks ago. I'm not a prudish person, but I found his language a bit excessive, especially over something as trivial as grass.

That's where he draws the line? Trees he worship but grass is what he considers silly? I wasn't able to ponder on this for too long as Shepard stood up, knocking back his coffee with a satisfied sigh.

Thank you. You have done a great deed today. I will be in touch.

And with that, he left. I tried to stop him. I tried to think of something to say or shout or do. I tackled someone for attempting to kick my dog, but I couldn't bring myself to say anything when it was a person! A dickhead, yes, but still a person all the same. Seconds later Shepard was gone, and I was left with a sickening feeling in my stomach, that my body had betrayed me. I've heard people have felt this way when they soil themselves in war or have become aroused in inappropriate moments; a feeling reminding us just how alien we are to ourselves. Strange thinking nothings inside a goopy organ inside a boney cage wrapped in swads of fat, muscle, and veins beneath a blanket of skin and hair and constraints. Masters of our movements, slaves of our biology. I stood there, alone, wondering what part of me forced the suggestion from the recesses of my mind, up into my throat, and stumbling through my mouth. Anger? Fear? Malice? My coffee was long cold when I was able to go on about my day.

It was Halloween night, technically the first of November, All Soul's Day, when I received a message on my phone. I wasn't long gone to sleep, or at least trying to sleep. My burst of spontaneity was still playing on my mind. I was easily stirred fully awake by the drum of the vibration and sudden glow of the screen, singeing my eyes as they shot open. I was glad for the distraction, I thought at the time, because I was growing frustrated with tossing and turning this way and that way. Even Diva, nesting between my legs, was grateful for the momentary break from this night-time chore. I reached for my phone and read the notification. A video message from an unknown number.

The sickening feeling from before had surged back into my gut, churning bile with boiling anxiety. I tried to soothe myself, telling myself I didn't know what the video was. That was a lie. As though I had gained precognition, I knew. There was no point fooling myself. I was neither stupid nor fortunate. Ordinarily, I'm sure you'd agree, a video from an unknown caller would go unread if not outright deleted. It sounds like the kind of scam a hapless idiot or your mother would fall for. On this occasion, though, given the recent visit from Shepard, it seemed pertinent. I should have tried going to sleep instead. I opened the message and played the video.

It was dark. Huge splodges of black and dark grey pixels filled the screen. A roaring crackle and hiss gave the impression, along with the darkness, that the scene was taking place outside. The videographer, whoever they were, wrestled to keep the shaky video stable, flashing frozen instances in time; barely lit feet, a patch of dim grass, the shattered shards of moonlight through tree branches. Finally, the frame rate caught up with itself, though still a difficult to parse standard definition twenty-five FPS. I felt like it was 2007 again. The "improved" quality clarified the audio. There were the persistent cars shushing along the distant motorway, the cool whistle of the night air, the soft collapse of tattered grass, and something else. Something unusual. It sounded like talking, yet there were no words; none intelligible anyway.

The camera panned up, revealing a submerging depth of red aura; bulbous orbs of heat, each with a blistering, over-exposed centre, held at the end of wood sticks high in the air by an army of shadowy minions. At the front of this crowd holding fiery torches, I could just make out the sharp features, jagged though they were, of Shepard, holding up his hands, staged dramatically before the shot. Raising up high above him was a shaking and squirming mass, like a boil or wart, seemingly out of place with the rest of the ladder it was strapped to. The video tracked forward, getting in closer to the restrained mass. The noise got louder and a little clearer, though still indistinguishable. With the flicker of the fire aiding the poor quality, enough highlights were defined for me to recognise Euen, the park ranger, strapped, bound, and gagged to a ladder, being slowly manoeuvred towards the paddock of trees.

I jolted out of bed, thinking I could stop them, but I quickly remembered this was a video and not a live stream. He was probably long gone now. As I watched, helpless to stop them feeding him to the trees, I finally made out what his muffled screams were.

GET OFF THE GRASS! GET OFF THE GRASS!

XIII.

I don't know if I believe in anything after death. I think there's something, like a god or something, but not in the "God" sense. I can imagine people going to Heaven, but never myself. I don't think I don't deserve it, I just can't see myself in Heaven, no more than I can see myself in space; I can visualise it, but I'm left wondering where the punch-line is . Thanatophobia; that's what I have. I'm not going to Hell and that scares me. I know it must seem strange; there are trees driving people mad, killing them, driving them to suicide, yet I can't bring myself to believe in an afterlife? Yes. Faith, even in nothing, isn't rational.

The reason why I find myself introspective on the matter is because of a visit I received from a new face in the village. There was a knock at the door. I have no idea why everyone knocks. I do have a doorbell! Diva immediately goes off and I start swearing at her to shut it. I was half expecting to find Shepard but instead I was surprised by a woman, a little younger than myself, standing there, in a nice business suit, holding the handles of a black satchel.

Hello! I'm looking for a Mr...

She goes to check a note she pulls out of her pocket. I interrupt her, saying I'm who she's looking for. I had no way of knowing that for certain, but no one was going to just happen to knock on my door accidentally. The woman tucked the card back into her pocket and presented her hand for a handshake.

Good morning, I'm Natasha Grosset. I'm a communication officer with Intellex Processing. I was wondering could I speak to you about your experiences involving the trees in St. Catherine's Park?

Intellex Processing is a multinational corporation that has a sprawling campus in Leixlip. It's been rumoured for years they've been the cause of suspicious trends in the village since their arrival; growing cancer diagnoses, water contamination, employee disappearances, strange lights and smoke seen over their buildings. I don't buy into much of that. Seems like it's veering into conspiracy theory territory, but I don't trust anything without a face. There is no such thing as a good corporation, just an unprofitable one. Be that as it may, I agreed and welcomed Ms. Grosset in. Diva sniffed Natasha's heels and, placated, wandered into the kitchen and slept on one of the chairs.

I made us coffee (Natasha requested) and we began.

I hope you don't mind, but I'd like to start with a few statements. We're conducting an internal investigation and we'd appreciate anything you can tell us.

I didn't say it, but I knew this was a half-lie. How is it internal if you have to look outside your own company? No, I'd say this was to see was there anything anyone had seen that connected them to the trees. I didn't think they had anything to do with them, but if I was them, with all that money and reach, I'd want to make sure as well.

I began to tell her everything. The trees, the first person I witnessed going into them, the people coming, the tree out the back (which had now completely covered the windows so much you can't even see the back, let alone get out to it), Mary, Shepard, the cult. None of it phased her. She just continued to write it on a notepad from her satchel, in short-hand, whipping to new pages with a disinterested flick of her hand. She didn't glance up at me once, most likely considering briefly the inconsequential words before moving on.

I made us fresh coffee just before the topic moved onto myself; more personal statements. Do I believe in love? How long have I known about my sexuality? What's my answer to the trolley problem? And, to bring it back to the start, do I believe in an afterlife? That was the one I didn't answer. I said I couldn't. Natasha said that was okay. From her sigh, her tired smile, and the way her hand lay flat on top of the closed notepad, I got the impression I had given her nothing to further investigate. Maybe she knew all this already. Maybe other people had been interviewed before me.

I was seeing her out with Diva finally coming around, circling Natasha, fawning for belly scratches, when Natasha said something that jogged my memory.

Well, thank you again for the coffee. If you think of anything else that might be of interest, you can phone reception and ask for my extension.

The mental image of the man in white, peering out from the trees, came racing back to me. I mentioned it just as Natasha had stepped outside and I was standing at the front door. I expected her to just quickly jot it down on her notepad. What happened instead was Natasha's polite smile dropped, fading as quickly as the colour from her face and the pupils from her eyes.

I thought you said it was a woman you saw go in first!

I clarified what I meant; that the man was in the paddock, looking out. She pressed me grillingly.

And are you SURE they were inside the paddock? Do you mean they were beside the wall? Did you see them go over the wall or were they definitely inside it already?

I tried to stay calm, but the panic in her voice was unsettling. Nonetheless, I reiterate what I said; I saw a man in white looking out from over the wall, under the trees, from within the paddock. I asked was something wrong.

.... No...

That was all I got. A ghostly, vacant single word, like the escaping breath of death. It was soft. It was scared. She left with no farewell. All I got to remember this strange encounter was a nagging question on my mind; what do I believe?

XIV.

It's Christmas in a few days, and understandably there's an unease about it. There's an odd feeling of shame intermingled with determined jovial spirits. There are fewer houses than ever decorated (many are without the excuse of being abandoned), yet of those that are, they appear more festive than in previous years. Interestingly, many of the ones I know lie empty are decorated, draped in lights hanging from the gutters, windows frosted in mock-snow from a spray can, and, perhaps a little morbidly given everything, a tree dressed in baubles and lights. Fake trees, obviously, but you wouldn't blame people for breaking from tradition.

Even myself and Diva made the point of erecting our own everlasting evergreen, hanging memories of years gone; ornaments marked "2017" or photos encapsulated within spheres. There's a photo of me and my late partner smiling at a Christmas display at Dublin Zoo. Another one is of two penguins with our names written on their bellies. I've even seated the stuffed teddies she used to insist I put on the tree, all eight of them. I try not looking at it for too long so I don't get overwhelmed.

I had fallen asleep on the sofa, with the last of the cooling radiator's heat, the soft aura of the lit tree, and the low volume of the lofi streaming from the TV lulling me into peace. Diva was nestled between my knees and atop the blanket covering my legs. I must have dozed off in the middle of reading "Dubliners", for it was in my hands when Diva had awoken me, growling as she spoke.

Wake up! Wake up, Dennis!

I knew I was dreaming because my name is not Dennis. I sat upright, lifting myself higher. Diva, sitting up but still in between my knees, was dragged along with the blanket.

This has been going on for too long, James. We must make preparations.

I agreed with her, though I asked her to not call me James, which was not my name either. I knew what she meant, though, even in my dream. The trees, the disappearances, the cult; it's all been going on for a little over a year now. I had hoped my new found compliance would at least signal some kind of outlet, an opportunity to escape presenting itself or a way to position myself in more favourable circumstances, but nothing seemed to be on the horizon. I had no promise Shepard wouldn't come after me. I tried explaining this to Diva.

Listen to me, Mary!

I'm starting to think my dog doesn't understand the concept of names.

I may not get this opportunity to speak to you on the matter again. Not in English, at least. You know this Shepard person is not good. I believe you humans would call him a "fanatic". But you are underestimating the danger he places all of us in, especially you and me, Peter!

Still not my name.

Men like that, men of devotion, are men of preconception. They do not react well to reality. They devote themselves to wishes, not tides of chance. He doesn't just see the world a certain way, he lives in a world he wills it to be. He is not living in a world where the trees swallow people; he lives in a movie where he is the hero. You, Philip, as the Tree Guy, threaten that. But to outright kill you is to go against his narrative; at least without a better excuse than jealousy, for the time being.

How my dog can understand the concept of Narrative Identity Theory, but not my name, I don't know.

Listen to me Sinead; you are only "The Witness" so long as you are useful to him. You bolster his ego as a messiah of sorts. Once you can no longer serve that function, you will be disposed of. Be weary. Do not grow complacent. It is better to reign in Hell than to serve in Heaven. When the time comes, you must know there is every likelihood one of you will need to kill the other. You may be able to live without doing so, but I fret Shepard will be incapable. I may never get another chance to warn you, so please heed my words. Also, if this is the one chance I get, there is something else you must remember. Do you know the way you scratch my belly and ask me "Who's my woo-woo girl? Who's my special woo-woo girl?"

Yes?

Please continue that. I enjoy it very much.

That was the one and only time Diva ever spoke to me. It's also the one time she turned out to be correct; one of us would indeed kill the other.

XV.

If I said you were invited to a party, but I said it with a gun in my hand, would you go even if you didn't want to? I've always found it funny whenever I received a letter from the Department of Social Protection, welfare that is, proclaiming how I am invited to an exciting employment activation scheme… or else I may have my jobseekers allowance cut. They never outright say it, but it's heavily implied. My theory is they can't outright say they will cut it. Likewise, me holding a gun isn't me threatening you, but you probably should accept the invitation.

Death and taxes, they say, are the only certainties in life. I think they missed bureaucracy. When I think of the time I blurted out that park ranger's name when Shepard was looking for a sacrifice, I knew for certain I had lost my mind because it never occurred to me to name someone from the department. Even before my partner passed away, they were hounding me. They had gone quiet when the trees first gained notoriety, but I should have known better than to think that would have lasted long. I wonder, did they too, like many in the country, lose someone to that cursed paddock, or do soulless creatures of eldritch horror not attract? Does Real recognise Real? After everything, the deaths, the mania, the breakdowns still going on, they're once again inviting people. I had no choice.

The "Job-Way" Reactivation Centre was located in the Maynooth Business Park, an ironic misnomer since it was located outside of Maynooth. Whoever named it obviously didn't have to walk the forty minutes to get to it from the train station, off the bridge, down past the petrol station, past the large gated homes, past the last bus stop in Maynooth, past another petrol station, past the small estate still under-construction, past the Aldi (or was it a Lidl?), over the bypass, dodging speeding cars turning onto or off the M4 motorway, crossing the three-lane road, following the path around the corner into the entrance of the business park, and then following the main road until you reached Building F.

I was just about to head on inside, grabbing the door handle and reading the floor layout to learn that Job-Way was in Room A on the ground floor, when I saw, to my disbelief, a tree in the car park. But not just any tree. This tree was just like the one in my back garden. The longer I stared, the more I was beginning to convince myself it was the exact same tree, not just a similar one. It only then occurred to me that I had heard of something like the trees in the paddock before. At the time, the name escaped me, but I've since learned it's called Pando; a single organism that connects a forest of trees, as though they were conjoined twins. This factoid struck me at the moment. What else struck me was the realisation that the tree's presence didn't bode well for those at Job-Way. Perhaps, I thought morbidly as I entered, the trees were good for something after all.

We, myself and the unfortunate invitees, were sitting in a little side presentation room, across from the makeshift receptionist desk. A Power Point presentation was on the screen, displaying a collection of regurgitated platitudes about seizing the day, living your best life, and other buzzwords at least half a decade old that have only now seeped into corporate consciousness; unsurprising when you learn Job-Way is run by a private agency, Settex, who makes money by low-balling government contracts, profiting off taxes, and getting people off the dole by any means, so their taxes can go to them too. Their parent company also happens to be Intellex Processing. Like I said; eldritch horror.

The lights dimmed and music started playing; a loop of a synth melody escalating to a double beat. Myself, the too-young-to-retire-sixty-year-old, the housewives looking to get back out there, and the Polish graphic designers were all looking around us, confused. The door erupted, and a man rushed past us, spinning in mid air and landed spread legged, holding out his hands, with the most horrifically American smile you've ever seen.

GOOOOOOOOOD MORNING! ARE YOU READY-

They clapped their hands together, further puncturing the stunned silence.

-TO GET BACK TO LIVING!

Sweet Jesus, I think I figured out what Shepard did before the trees! This, it would turn out to be, was Fredrick Paulton, who insisted we called him Freddio, joking, I hope, that he wouldn't answer to anything else, before chuckling to himself. Fredrick was the kind of man who was in his forties but desperately saw himself as a thirty-something-year-old. His relatively fit body, rolled up sleeved shirt, and neatly combed quaff on his aged yet hairless face, along with his bombastic entrance, gave the distinct impression that he bought into motivational speakers like Tony Robbins. I don't disparage that, but not everything can be solved with the power of confidence. No one is in a wheelchair because of a bad attitude. No one was touched as a kid because they didn't have a dream board. No one dies of rectal cancer because they had negative thoughts. Fredrick would disagree.

We sat there for an hour as Fredrick talked through the presentation. According to Job-Way, we weren't unemployed; we were Prospective Workers. They weren't employment agents; they were Career Activators. And we weren't forced to sign contracts that gave away our data; we were joining the patented Job-Way Honesty Family. The only interruption to Fredrick's speech was when he asked two men in the row in front of me why they were talking. One explained his friend spoke no English, and he was translating. Fredrick allowed this, getting back to his speech on why there was no reason we couldn't have jobs.

Afterwards, we were assigned our Career Activators. Some people called out on a roll call were missing. I recognised some as names of people who were swallowed by the trees. It is curious why their names would still be on the register, unless someone was still claiming their allowances. Fredrick got around to my name. I held up a hand, forcing back an "anseo!" from habit. Fredrick smiled, for it was my ill fortune that he was my Career Activator.

I was told to sit at his desk. The office space itself was small enough where only six other agents could work. Whoever wasn't up for a discussion was made to use the ten computers we would be using for job searching. Fredrick kept me waiting about ten minutes, as he had managerial duties to carry out first (guiding his fellow bullshitters, having no patience for those invitees who were computer illiterate, denying us reimbursed travel costs despite the fact the letter said they would be). As he finished up, from the uncomfortable stackable seat next to his more inviting swivel chair, I saw the tree again outside through the window. I could swear it looked closer than it was when I first saw it. Finally, Fredrick sat down. I politely hummed in passive compliance as he began another spiel about being here to help, ending with;

So... why do you think you're unemployed?

I've never understood this question. It's like asking why do you think you're sick? Why am I suddenly expected to know? Maybe there is a certain level of responsibility you must accept, but it can never be complete. How am I to account for chance and randomness, to respond succinctly with all the nuances of economic effects on the work force? I'm not supposed to; that's the point. It's not a question, it's an assault on personhood. I did my best. I talked about how I believed my issue was an internalised shame from being a promising student in school with some creative ambitions but failed to launch successfully after graduation. Little by little, my confidence and self-worth were chipped away. One year becomes two, becomes five, becomes ten. Despite the odd jobs, part time work, and emigration, you are registered as unemployed until you have a full-time job, even if you're not on the dole, so even if you get work, it counts for nothing. It wore away at me. Eventually, you start wondering what's the point. All those dreams, those hopes, they fade away. What's the point of anything? And then there are the trees. I can't blame them. In a way they ground you. They pull back the illusion. Why would I want a job if my boss would replace me tomorrow? Who can think about working when death is everywhere? How is anyone supposed to not be affected by any of this?

Fredrick throatily groaned.

Okay, I hear you... but why wouldn't you want to work?

I didn't respond. I was silent from expectant bemusement, not dumbfoundedness. Thankfully Fredrick ignored me and continued explaining how Job-Way would work. I was to report back weekly and use the computers to search for jobs for at least one hour. Your taxes at work; babysitting adults. You voted for this.

As I left, disgruntled as I wasn't reimbursed for the train, I looked to the right to check on the tree. I was right; it had moved. Just like the tree in my back garden, it seemed to have wafted closer, gliding through nothing. My initial gleeful thought earlier that the tree would act out a karmic retribution on my behalf now felt in bad taste. They were monsters, yes, but only on a human level. They didn't deserve to die. Tragically, one of them would.

XVI.

The following week, when I returned to fulfil my new obligations I was so generously invited to partake in, walking once again from the train station, passed the two petrol stations, and playing a real life game of Frogger across the bypass, and then the length of the business park, I found the tree had moved so close to the building that it was now pressing up against it. The branches were splayed out like fingers, stretching up the wall, sprawling in fractal veins, digging into the dips and divots of the brick. Once I entered, I saw the walls had shallow cracks just barely breaking through the paint. I hated these people, but I had to say something. I had failed to help so many already. Even if it wasn't my fault, I'm dying inside with the guilt, the shame of being helplessly human.

But Fredrick didn't care. He just shuffled over to me on the computer and asked why do I think I haven't found work yet. I did a double take, caught off-guard by the nonchalance, briefly wondering was I back in last week again. I shook it off and tried in vain to tell him about the tree outside, about how I've seen trees just like it devour people in their own gardens, and how he needed to relocate the offices.

Right, right, I hear you, buddy! But maybe this is what's holding you back from stepping up in life; worrying about other people. Now, this is just a thought, but why don't you try not doing that?

It was the same the following week. The only difference was the tree was now penetrating into the building. The branches swooped up high above the body and curved into the wall, as though in the night it had swung a punch and planted a hit into the wall. The branches held themselves steady, like bark covered pipes. The little spindles of twigs now reached the top of the building, interweaving around one another, like the tails of a rat-king, gripping the exterior in a mesh. The inside was no better, as the branches piercing through the walls lined the ceiling like support beams. Drips of sap fell, forming puddles beneath. I tried my best to skirt around them, tightening my scarf as I still felt the cold cascading in through the broken windows, thick branches having caused cracks and shattered openings. The receptionist, who was still refusing to pay anyone's travel fare, forced a smile while she tried to keep her hands warm despite still wearing her coat. Fredrick seemed to take offence at this, shouting over to her that there was nothing to be done about the temperature until the radiators were fixed.

I took a different approach. Before Fredrick could finish his monologue about how he's here to help me help myself, I cut across him, stating bluntly that he was going to die. The clatter of the keyboards died away, leaving just my soft voice and the hush of the cold January wind through the openings. I told him he was going to be dead this time next week, if not sooner, if he didn't relocate the offices. Go anywhere, I told him. Literally anywhere else. I didn't care. I didn't care about the rent, the contracts, the dole. I didn't care about Fredrick, and I told him so, but I pleaded with him to just leave this building and save his own life.

Fredrick nodded. He hummed. I have never had as sweet a breath of relief as in that fleeting, flickering second that I thought I had gotten through to him. Then he opened his mouth.

I just want to thank you for that. It was really something.

SWEET JESUS!

Really, I want you to know I am hearing you loud and clear. That...

He pointed at me.

That really struck a chord with me... In here...

He turned his extended finger in on to himself.

And I want to say I hear you, I see you, but most importantly, I acknowledge you.

There was a pen to the side of the computer's keyboard. Would a ball-point pen be strong enough to stab someone in the jugular, I wondered.

Your experience is valid and I recognise that. I appreciate your truth.

I mean, even if the pen breaks off, you can still stab again with the cracked end, right?

You have really gifted me with a lot. We are on the same journey, with different paths.

The real question is whether after breaking the shard had enough tensile strength to not break again... I was beginning to think the only way to be certain would be to follow through with my thoughts.

But... I do have just one tiny question...

This man dies. I'm only telling you ahead of time because you know where this is going.

...Why do you feel...

Just end it there, please! Why do I feel? I ask myself that every day!

...the need to not look after yourself? Like in having a job, for example.

I didn't say much after that. I gave enough of a response for him to leave me alone. I did my hour, occasionally eye the pen, and left, knowing full well what I would be walking into the following week. It still took me by surprise, though.

Down the road, past the petrol stations, nearly getting hit by a lorry, and then... I stopped at the entrance of the business park. From this distance I could clearly make out Building F, now wrapped in constricting branches and a twisting trunk, bespeckled by leaves. In the faint overcast light I could still see the sheen of the oozing sap, trickling down the building, coating it in a syrup of honey gold, dark and dirty in clumps large enough to make out even from here. The parking spaces outside were a dishevelled minefield of jagged pieces and exposed pipes, torn up by waves of roots, along with a small woodland of trees, dispersed across the radius of the building, slowly but surely making their way to the centre, as though they were baby spiders called for their matricidal feast.

Once inside, I could see the thin carpet had been engorged by a thick decay of leaves, squelching with each step, gurgling mucky bubbles beneath my soles. The overhead branches hung lower now, lank and slack. The walls and fixtures on them were painted in a glacially slow downpour of sap, uneven and clumping in places. The door into the Job-Way offices was torn off its hinges by tiny vines creeping through the walls, which seemed to breathe shallowly under the sap. No one was here... except for Fredrick.

Fredrick was directly in front of me as I entered, bound to his comfortable swivel chair by coiling branches snaking across his limbs, slipping under his clothes, tearing through his skin and bones. His head, white and balding, with little colour other than the disturbingly vibrant purple of his veins, was held in place by a snare of branches, violating his orifices, holding his mouth agape. Just one bulging eye was exposed, the pupil pushing the whites to the fringes.

I'm sorry Fredrick. I'm sorry there's people like you in the world. It would be merciful if you didn't exist. I turned to the computers, broken and repurposed as little terrariums, moss spilling out from the towers and screens. They almost looked pleasantly quaint. There was no point staying. I made my way to the receptionist's desk and forced open the money box; I was owed twenty euros for travel fare. When I went for the door, I heard a forced, struggling cry from behind me.

Why...

I looked around at Fredrick. The only movement from his mouth was his tongue, floundering like a dying fish giving feeble, anguished jerks.

Why...

I pity them; oblivious to how insignificant we are. As soon as I left, I was sure the trees would descend upon him and do whatever they wished. I didn't feel bad for taking the money, nor for leaving him, but I did for not being able to answer him. I didn't know why. I still don't. As I exited through the door, I heard the last thing he may have ever said.

Why?

XVII.

My hair was becoming shaggy and untamed when I finally decided it was time to get a cut. I take after my mother; dark, wavy, thick, and wild when it's left alone, especially with comb resistant bed head. I put off the hair cut mainly because of the prices these days.

I left the barbers, passing abandoned shop fronts on the dying Main Street, debating with myself whether to buy some food from the Aldi built where an old pub used to be or if I should just cook what I have at home, when I heard a cough, weak and wheezy, behind me. I turned around, finding Shepard, though it took me a moment to recognise him. Without a crowd around him, he appeared less expansive and commanding, almost unhealthily thin. His starved figure was only further accentuated by the nervous way he pulled his coat in around himself, as though embarrassed he was in public. He even looked around the quiet road, as if worried someone would see him. I compensated for his seeming insecurity by informally asking how was he doing. He darted a glance at me.

May we talk?

The question only furthered the surreality here. This is a man who forced his way into my life, bringing a whole community into his quasi-religious obsession, bombarding us with made up verses (I checked), and has thrown people to whatever mind-bending madness exists in the paddock behind those piled stones, and here he is, formally asking if we may speak. I asked what did he want to speak about.

Are you busy, Witness? Are you heading home?

The internal debate abruptly resolved itself. Yes, I was heading home to cook what I call "Elevated Beans on Toast" (baked beans cooked with Mexican hot sauce atop toasted bread spread with English mustard, with a gooey sunny-side-up fried egg capping everything, littered with grated cheddar). Shepard seemed enthused by this, as though he was hoping to come in. He can forget that; I'm not cooking for two.

I'll walk with you. We can talk, if you don't mind.

It was strange to see, really, for the first time, just how normal Shepard was when he had no audience. He was boring, in fact. A good two or three heads taller than myself, though not exactly difficult, he was brought closer to my height by a prominent slouch, his gangly arms squirrelling away into his coat pockets. His aged good looks were drastically at odds with this adolescent level of awkwardness. It must have looked funny to see us so mismatched. I was unusually chatty, trying to fill up the silence, goading Shepard into speaking, remarking that I could tell something was wrong. This must have cut his ego slightly because he tried to return to form.

Those called to serve are never untested. The instruments of deeds can not be left to rust nor go blunt... but I confess...

Shepard's efforts deflated beneath their own loftiness, unable to fully commit to the bit.

I am growing... worried. I- We, that is, were called to be part of wonders, bringing forth a New Eden. It seemed so simple in the beginning. We would thank the trees. We would pray to them. Love them. But then I was called to do more. To recruit. To teach. To feed. To cook. To present. And then there was you.

I pretended, as we walked up the steep Captains Hill, to not notice the harshness forcing out that last sentence.

I did not know it then why would the trees favour you. Our members who are guards told me how you were the one the trees showed themselves to, how you were "The Tree Guy". They came for you in your garden. They wished for you to join them. And I must admit I was... perhaps... a little jealous.

My sarcastic exclamation of shock was lost on Shepard, who answered sincerely.

Oh yes! It is true! I knew what I was meant to do. I was to bring another piece of the New Eden into place, ensuring our future paradise would be solidified. But now I am tested once more. I tell you this because I know you will not tell anyone.

Who the Hell do I have to tell? Diva?

I have remained faithful. I have continued to feed them, but I have noticed they hunger still. They are still going into people's houses. I have heard they have even travelled as far as Maynooth. Imagine; they may reach the midlands or the border within a year. I have noticed there is one, in the very centre, growing.

Now my joyful savouring for Shepard's discomfort morphed into genuine concern as I asked him what did he mean by growing. He reiterated.

Growing. Tabitha noticed it first. I scolded her for what I believed was deceit and a lack of faith. She was sick for a fortnight after we made her sleep outside, but then I noticed it too. What's more, while the surrounding trees are seasonal, still without their spring buds, this central tree is strangely a lone evergreen. Stranger still is how it's... it looks like it's leaning, as though growing at an arc.

The further along the route home we took, the further into this confessional we continued, the more concerned I was becoming with these new details, but also the more I became aware that Shepard would be getting to his point that would concern me soon.

I have a confession to make to you. I came to you before, wishing you to name a sacrifice. And you did so. I must compliment you. But, as with the all-seeing eye of our trees, I have sight to observe. No one savours in toiling, of course, but I couldn't help but notice you were drained of the experience. It is exhaustive work, as I can attest. So I decided to choose the next person. I intended to return to you, but I was worried you would refuse. I can appreciate your lack of constitution.

Did he just call me a pussy?

But I couldn't take that risk. Contrary to our limited interactions, I do like you. While my flock are loyal, they are compared to sheep for a reason. Before I was called, I believed the religious were ungifted in critical thought. Perhaps a sinner like I was has some wisdom. You, however, are astute. Patiently stoic. A lesser man would have left months ago.

A lesser man in that case would have the money to do so.

Shepard burst into a bark of laughter, startling me. I didn't realise I had said that out loud.

Yes! Man and his money, eh? A beggar asks for your money; a rich man simply takes it. Well, my point is I didn't wish to force myself upon our relationship. But there was little point even if I did, for the trees called for more. And then more. And more after that. Even if you were willing, you would have been out-paced by them. I took it upon myself to choose. Even now, my flock is persuading others to go in, by insistent methods if required. We made a unique discovery in the process. In between some sacrifices, there were longer periods of time where the trees were quiet. These satiated periods always came after a sacrifice where the person involved was deeply mourned. Parents, children, partners. So my- excuse me, our theory is that, though it sounds flowery and sentimental, love can be tasted, like it would be in a meal or in a gift. This sense of emotion, of human feeling, is what we believe the trees actually feed on, what they need to be appeased. Which brings us to your dog, Diva.

I halted in place immediately, my legs stalling rigidly. The full weight of realisation reverberated throughout my body. It wasn't of fear, however. I felt overcome by insulted fury and disgusted anger that Shepard, who too froze, realising his mistake, would even dare to put forward the idea that I would let anyone harm my Diva, my baby. I spoke as restrained as I could.

If you ever come near my dog, I will beat your face in so badly your cracked teeth will shred the inside of your throat as you choke on them. I will cave in your skull to protect Diva, even if I have to do it with the worn away stubs of my broken wrists. I will leave you in the dirt soiling yourself, bleeding out, and gurgling for the release of death. Do we understand each other?

Shepard took his time to answer.

No.

I left him there, heading on home without another word, making sure that night to double check all the doors and windows were locked, the alarm was set, and to cuddle Diva extra tight in bed as we fell asleep. I would, and did, murder for Diva.

XVIII.

I did something stupid. Illuminating, but stupid. I suppose that's the same for most people; moments of clarity in drips and drabs of the unintentional. The situation with the trees, for instance. It's peculiar how things have only dawned on me in retrospect. The initial researchers all arrived in Intellex Processing vehicles and gear when the mystery of the trees first occurred. We all just assumed they were from the government. All the research they collected, therefore, was privately owned, and thus could benefit no one. Information that could save lives kept secret.

But then it occurred to me; there's nothing stopping me from going down to the park myself and doing my own research. I'm not a scientist, but at this point, anything was better than nothing. Even if I learned one thing, it would have been worth the experiment. Besides, as things were going, I felt an impasse was approaching. It would serve me well to be a little more knowledgeable, I thought.

So Diva and I left for the park. She needed her walk anyway, but, ever since Shepard's indecent proposition, I've taken to leaving Diva alone as little as possible. I have to laugh; she still barks going out. Usually she'd be answered by a chorus of estate dogs yapping from their gardens, but there aren't many left, either fleeing with their families or simply taken by the trees. Diva's barks are met by a distant yip, carried by the wind from somewhere in Riverforest. But we're not heading that way.

Spring has finally arrived, bringing with it the conflict of sun, soft clouds, skyward seas of lapis, and strong gusts swaying the bare but soon to be budding branches. I love seeing the same in Autumn, when the blossom petals flitter down in a dusting of pink and peach. How our walks used to be; that's what keeps us going. A wish for reversal, a Faustian bargain to relive a past we never wish to escape.

We pass the old monastery, turn the corner, heading for the pitches, obliterated in the absence of the park ranger, and make our way to the trees. Two things catch our attention. First, like Shepard mentioned, there was indeed a noticeably large evergreen right in the centre of the thick woodland. It wasn't like a redwood, which would simply stretch with a narrow span. In fact, there was no taper at the top. Even though it was just peaking over the height of the other trees, what you could see gave the impression that it was fat and stocky, like a pyramid. If it was growing, it may have been a sapling when I saw the man behind the wall that night. Even that has a haze of longing for us now. And second, once our eyes drifted down to the paddock walls, we found a small congregation kneeling, apparently praying to the trees. I saw no tall, good looking man, but I did make out the squat, bulbous form of his assistant, Tabitha.

Nonetheless, we didn't slow down our approach, and, about a few yards from them, Tabitha, at the front of the group conducting the mumbling symphony, finally noticed us. The members, realising a shift in her focus, joined her in watching me and Diva strut up the pitch. Slowly, they all stood up to witness our magnificent energy. Tabitha stepped out from the group, holding herself to her fullest height, which wasn't much, planting her feet on the ragged earth. She went to speak, but neither of us stopped. She stuttered and fell silent once we side-stepped her on our way to the sloping trench.

The sloping trench was an undergrowth of strangled weeds, pillowy moss, discarded litter, and, fortunately for us, broken twigs. The blanket of leaves from the previous year which buried the trench in a heavy brush had broken down enough where the treasures we sought laid exposed, like shipwrecks on a shore. Diva sniffed around, leaping from mossy patch to mossy patch delightfully as I studied what was on offer. I wasn't too sure what I was hoping for, but I figured something about the length of my hand, narrowing to an uncut tip, with some offshoots, would have been ideal. Not too long, not too short, varied, but replicable. Once I spotted the perfect one, I simply plucked it up, turned around to Tabitha and others, gave them the finger, and strut past.

I must admit, once we were home, I wasn't exactly sure what to do. The motivation at the start was more on a whim, born from disappointment. So much had gone wrong, so I thought why not? Shits and giggles. There's only so far you can push someone before they crack.

Detaching Diva from her harness with my right hand, I held up the twig to what little light was making its way into the front hall. As I said, it was a bland twig, as uniform and weak as a chicken bone. I turned it between my fingers as I walked into the kitchen, hanging my coat on the back of the chair by the table. I leaned on the chair, still studying the twig. I swore to myself, realising I had tricked myself into the most boring project imaginable. Well... if I was to suffer in lobotomising boredom, I should make myself a coffee at least to keep me awake.

I had turned my back on the twig on the table for only a brief second, selecting an Americano Grande pod to insert into the machine. But when I turned back around, the twig was gone.

Fuck!

Diva was in the front room, most likely sleeping on the sofa, so it's not like she saw where it went. As the coffee machine sprang into life, nasally whining, I got down on my hands and knees. I crawled along, hovering my head off the floor just enough to look under the oven and the fridge, both narrow caverns of dust and dirt, discarded bottle caps, and the odd twenty cent coin. Pawing and shuffling forward, I search under the chairs, the table, the kitchen dresser, and even the radiator. Still nothing.

The coffee machine hissed steam and sputtered the last drops from the pod as I gave up, scratching my head. Diva was standing in the open doorway to the hall as I stood up, looking at me as if to wonder what I was doing. I wondered the same myself. Stumped, I reached for my coffee and took a big gulp.

The bastard was hiding in the cup, swimming around in the dark, mucky depths, waiting for the right time to spring out and latch onto the back of my throat. My cup fell, smashing into large shards, thumping my toes, stabbing into the soles of my feet, and scalding my skin in a sticky filament. I didn't feel any of that at the moment, because I was far too distracted by the capillary sized shoots injecting themselves into my body. Conflicting gasps of shock, gags to vomit, and a hushed screech of pain pushed me back, stumbling over my steps, dropping to the ground, gripping my throat desperately. Over the rapid and deranged barks of Diva I could hear the twisting, churning sound of the twig growing shoots, evolving into an arboreal urchin. I felt these new additions seep through tissue. My neck was becoming stiff, pulled up and to the side with the strength to arch and lift my body off the ground. Was it trying to break my neck?

With bulging eyes, deafened ears, and animalistic fear, I plunged my fingers in between my teeth, frantically flicking and grabbing at whatever I could reach, grazing tiny limbs for the seconds that felt like torturous hours. I just managed to curl my middle finger around the body of the bastard, snagging on each of those appendages, gripping tightly at the surrounding walls. I nearly let go, flinching from the searing sting, but quickly came back to my senses. I knew this was going to be Hell to pull out. Even the twig realised this; I could feel it ease and slacken, an unsettling calm rippling disgustedly throughout my body. I imagine it thought it could lull me into letting go. Maybe if it hadn't been so aggressive.

One sweet, pleasant inhale. That's all I allowed myself.

My fingers curled tighter, flooding into a deep red from the strain. My free hand clasped around my other wrist, pulling the whole arm excruciatingly. Like tinnitus, I could hear the shredding of muscle, the leaking of blood, the strain of fibres, and the high pitch wail from within my being. Damned souls are easier to part with than this. I had the main body far enough out of my mouth for me to see it, yet there was still a weaving web of roots vanishing into my throat. My spine and arms ached, though I could not tell if this was from exhaustion or infection. I could hear the leathery tear from within so clearly my teeth winced and my skin pimpled.

One final tug, I whispered tenderly to myself.

One big, strong pull.

My hand shot out so quickly that if it wasn't for the pricking sensation numbing my palm, I would have thought I had accidentally flung the twig across the kitchen. In the brief seconds I had to observe the urchin, I saw it now resembled a tumble-weed, yet its strands and shoots didn't just splint off into an entropy of patterns but wrapped around themselves like barbed wire, tapered and bloated in places. Blood and strips clung to the ends, which looped back into the mass; a ball of ingrown hair hoping to leech off a host.

I could feel it once again, trying to get into my skin, hot and binding like wax. I grabbed it and tore it off, pulling up puckered punctured holes. Now it was attached to my left hand, refusing to be shaken off. This was becoming comical. In pain, shaking my hand wildly, I made my way to the dresser and clumsily searched the drawers, stealing glances to the tumble-weed sinking into my skin.

Finally! I found it!

I plunged the elongated neck of a lighter into the centre and clicked.

The urchin was set ablaze, burning with an even, spherical glow like a sun. My hand it slowly drifted upwards from was left unscorched. In fact, I instantly felt a refreshing wave of numbness, as though nothing had happened. Up higher it ascended, watched in awe by both me and the now silent Diva. Christ, it was magical. Imagine a floaty, those spots at the back of your eyes you can sometimes see, made real, only a shimmering molten neon orange. It would float higher and higher, passing through the ceiling, like a shadow in a fog.

I stood there, frozen for beats at a time before I jolted myself and scrambled upstairs, Diva skittering behind me. I forced open the stiff bedroom door just in time to see the ball pass through into the attic. I wasted no time rushing back down, out the front door, and across the road. We waited, watching the horizon of the rooftop for close to a minute before we saw it again, rising dreamily. We stood there watching its ascension for so long we lost track of whether we could still make out its glimmer or if it was one of the early stars peeking out in the slowly stewing evening sky.

No matter.

The trees could be killed, and their deaths were beautiful.

XIX.

It's easy to think there's only one outcome to events. Often the printing press is said to have brought about a new era in information, literacy, and free speech, but rarely is it mentioned how it privatised communication and mass-produced falsehoods. People will talk about how the fall of empires lead to the rise of nationalism, but never mention libertarianism, socialism, or democracy. We don't wish to admit good and bad or indifferent outcomes can share a source. In the same way, the trees caused people to join not just Shepard's cult. I found out on a seemingly "normal" Wednesday that there was another group forged from the birth of the trees.

I was returning from the local shop, complaining about the extortionist prices, begrudgingly enjoying my over-priced fizzy-drink when I heard it

Pssst!

I froze. It happened just at the back alley to the Riverforest shopping strip, where deliveries are made. It's a stretching road, abandoned besides the commercial-sized waste bins. It was from behind the nearest one, a recycling bin for the pub, that I heard it again.

Pssst!

I stared at it, waiting, rewarded with the peculiar sight of a man I've never seen before. Haggard and aged, though I got the impression younger than he looked, his prickly coat of grey beard contrasted against his long, stringy light brown hair, sadly not long enough to act convincingly as a comb-over, he slowly peered out, locking eyes with me. He searched around, throwing out another hiss for attention before darting back behind the bin again. This was Declan.

I asked was he talking to me.

WHAT! Shut up! Don't draw attention to yourself, ya thick!

I looked around; we were alone. Not difficult these days, even with March giving way for a pretty pleasant Spring.

Get over here!

I stalled, unsure, but this drained his patience quickly as he peered out once again and repeated his request. I walked over, my shopping swaying gently in my grip. I walked right around the other side of the bin, finding Declan crouched on the balls of his feet, his hands pressed against the side of the dumpster for support. It took him a moment to see me standing over him, confused. He jumped, asking me what the Hell did I think I was doing. I could have asked him that, seeing as it was he who told me to come over. He spat a quick barrage of insults.

Go stand on the other side! It looks suspicious otherwise!

Me reasoning we were past the point of suspicious didn't land with him, so I went back around the front. Satisfied his secret identity was safe, he introduced himself as Declan. He asked if I was the legendary Tree Guy. Besides being amused by the prefix "legendary", I wondered aloud why would he call me over if he wasn't even sure who I was.

...

The pause of silence confessed he hadn't thought this whole thing through, but continued, in what he thought was an encrypted code;

We meet half-four-night in the yard of courts.

It took me a second before I asked did he mean he wanted to meet tonight in the Courtyard Pub down the village.

...Yeah.

Now usually I don't accept invitations from strange men behind bins, asking me out for a drink at night, but I made the exception this once. I had not recognised Declan from the cult, which meant, if he was a local, at the very least he had no interest in Shepard's strange obsession, and, if he was hiding, he knew how much of a target that painted on him. Even the level of failed secrecy was a big indicator that, unlike the boldness of Intellex Processing, nor the obliviousness of those who had fallen victim to the trees, Declan was neither working for anyone nor was unaware of how serious things were. To be honest; I was intrigued. He never specified a time, so I guessed around eleven would be a good time to head down.

Walking down that night, I saw some cult members standing outside in the dark, down a cul-de-sac, watching me cross the road, turning their heads. I stopped in the middle of the road, staring down at the grouping of five, clumped together, illuminated in the amber street light. I noticed a glass bottle lying at the edge of a footpath curb. I picked it up and lobbed it at them, thinking it was funny when it struck one in the head, laughing as they yelled out. I was kept amused for the rest of the walk down into the village by that.

I entered through a side entrance from a car park because I didn't want to deal with the bouncer. Even with my beard, I wasn't in the mood to try explaining why I hadn't brought my passport. I'm sure Declan would have appreciated my covert inclination.

I wasn't expecting the pub to be completely deserted, but I was surprised to find a collection of men gathered around a table, hunched forward and low, struggling to stay together, as their chairs and stools blocked one another. They all dressed the same; Canada Goose jackets, bright blue jeans, and worn Nike runners. They ranged in age; as young as sixteen, as old as sixty. They were all white, too. That's not unusual for Ireland, but by contrast, Shepard's cult seemed more diverse. I must have stood there for some time since I heard a voice whisper.

Hey! Who's that lad?

They all turned around, facing me, a collage of faces through the life of a disappointing man staring back at me. Declan stood up, pulling himself away from his pack, shaking hands, and bringing me closer to the stern-faced men.

This, lads, is him! The Tree Guy!

This did little to appease them, though no one spoke any objection to my presence; some just returning to their huddle, whispering. Declan jostled me with his firm grip on my shoulder.

You're here just in time, lad. We were just about to head out and we'd like you to join us.

Before I could ask what was I in time for, the group, breaking apart, revealed stacked on the table a collection of Molotov-cocktails, petrol cannisters, lighters, matches, and deodorants. The men gathered up these items, shoving them into rucksacks and shopping bags. Declan, to my side, watched proudly. I asked what was happening.

They marched out of the side entrance, through the beer garden, past the bouncer, who pointed at me with an expression of annoyance, and down Main Street. Declan, escorting me with his grip upon my shoulder and elbow, explained as we went.

You see, Harry-

My name is not Harry.

-We are a group of concerned locals who just want to protect our community. You're one of us. You tried warning people before all this started. We figured you'd want to be involved it this. These trees have taken our children, our women, our jobs. Do you know what's really happening in the trees? Because we do. Do you know what's in there?

I waited. I wish he didn't go on.

Immigrants.

Yeah, that's just my luck. I'm hanging out with God Damn morons.

You see-

Oh, why is he still going on!

-The government is hiding refugees in the trees. That's what's happening. Foreigners are being shipped in and they're pretending the trees are doing these things, controlling the branches, breaking into people's houses. Hear about what happened in Maynooth? Did you know that there were Polish in that job centre? You can't say that's a coincidence!

Yes, you can.

What about those kids going in? See, it's the grooming gangs.

Christ.

They turn the boys into girls online and then get them into the trees. That's what's happening!

I feel conflicted hearing eejits like this. On one hand, they're stupid. But on the other, I do realise that they are just reacting to strange and scary circumstances far beyond their comprehension, lashing out with nonsensical rambling. That being said, they're still reactionaries who can get lost.

To my chagrin, Declan kept going as we pass the fire station and walked up a hill that led to the back entrance of the park.

Don't even get me started on the Feminists, Garth!

Again, not my name. And again, brain-rot.

You see, you and me are men. We're all men. The Woke want us to think being a man is a crime, "toxic". They'd rather we were weak and submissive. They'd rather take the kids and leave you for some black lad. I'm not racist, but we need to protect our people. So we're going to scorch the trees. Set them on fire. We're going to smoke the immigrants out and rescue our children. And then...

At first I thought Declan had realised how all this sounded. I thought maybe he could see that there's no end to conspiratorial thinking; there always has to be something in the shadows. But no. He had trailed off because a teenager ahead of us had lit their molotov.

What do you think you're doing, ya thick eejit!

Aren't we there!

No, ya wank stain! We're still like ten minutes off!

The teen, a boy of about sixteen, panicked and tossed it back down the hill, shattering at the base, spreading out into a sudden carpet of flames spanning the width of the road, shimmering in the night. As the smoke rose, everyone turned instinctively to the fire station, still visible only a few yards to our left.

SCATTER!

Amazingly, that came from me. We all hurried up the hill, not stopping until we were far enough down the plateaued road to not be seen by the firefighters, who, judging by the dying glow and the distant calls, were busy putting out the fire. In the reprieve, Declan, surprisingly calm, told the teenager to break into the water treatment plant, called the Shit Farm by locals, to see could he get any..."fuel". The poor lad was young and dumb enough to take him seriously, rushing off and over the gate, just happy to make up for his mistake. I felt sorry. I feel sorry for young people when they have men like Declan in their lives, cackling in the night, heading to try to set the trees on fire, thinking about nonsense.

Long before we made it to the pitch, the central evergreen I had seen last time was peeking out again, taller than ever, even from this distance, far down from the old monastery. It was no longer just the tip stretching above the others, but rather what looked like a green pyramid with a wide base, hiding its foundation behind the lesser surrounding trees. The March winds only further advanced the appearance that the Mega-Tree was bending forward, peering down on us fragile little humans. I don't like that thought; of it seeing us as dehumanised obstacles. I was worried Declan was rubbing off on me, like he had on the others we followed onto the pitch.

The group froze. Staring ahead of them, they saw Shepard's cult, gleefully clapping and celebrating as the branches wrapped around another victim, a sacrifice, carrying them up and over the paddock walls, screaming until they vanished into the darkness. It wasn't long before one of them noticed us staring at them, alerting the others. The stand off lasted only seconds before the molotovs were ignited, wasting time as the cult charged, stampeding forward, kicking up the ragged earth. By the time the group got moving, the cult had already taken up most of the pitch. Desperate, a few of the bottles were tossed too early, landing upon the soft dirt, pooling out with fiery puddles of mud and sugar-filled cheap vodka. I tried standing back, but the fight was soon surrounding me, forcing me to duck and dodge as I avoided being swept up, still getting knocked and pushed by the odd body stumbling into me or pair wrestling clumsily on the ground.

I looked up and saw the trees shake, rattling and hissing with the rustle of branches and leaves, pleased by the carnage. The pawing branches at the paddock walls beckoned the few cult members who had managed to subdue Declan's men and were dragging them closer, passing the shimmer of the fires. The heat and smoke choked the surrounding air so much one beer-bellied man, using a cannister to block punches, dosed the flames with a stream of petrol. The fire snaked up the spray and exploded in the cannister, knocking many onto their backs and sprinkling them in a splatter of flames, seeping into their jackets, jeans and hair, burning through. It was complete mayhem. The screams persisted as, trying to put out the flames or tear off their clothes, more of the men were dragged off to the trees, either tossed over the wall, silenced instantly, or else held up to the trees, their slithering branches coiling around the bodies and pulled them into their ranks, fading out their screams, like the last sounds before sleep. The Mega-Tree... I saw it grow.

Declan was no where to be seen. Perhaps he was already gone. I ran. I was lucky no one had taken notice of me, not even the squat silhouette of what I was sure was Tabitha, nor those few lucky enough to escape alongside me, running back down the hill, passing the monastery. I slowed down, watching the others run ahead. Passing the shit farm, the teenager who was sent in, now covered head to toe in a thick coat of excrement, like a nightmarish snowman, calling out to the others, wondering what happened. I explained. All I got was a subdued exclamation of surprise.

Oh.

I looked back, seeing no one else was following. It was only us who managed to escape. I really don't know what they expected. I turned back to the boy, ignoring the repulsive stench, and offered to walk him home. He did most of the talking along the way.

I was really looking forward to tonight! I just, you know, I just wanted to help, and do something... some friends of mine are in there.

Sometimes I see they're online in the chats. Ma says it's a glitch, but it's not like she knows.

I asked did his mother know he was out tonight. No answer. No answer either when I asked what about his father. I figured I might as well ask the only question he would be willing to answer; why join these lads?

...Why not? At least they're doing something. Guards do nothing. School does nothing. Grown ups don't care about lads like me. So why not? Decky, you know, Declan, guys like him at least do something. They try. People call him a thick or a racist, but I don't see them doing something.

The rest of the walk home was quiet enough, but his remarks stuck with me all the way home to my own bed in the wee hours of the morning, as the chill of the night met the early rays of the sunrise. Yes. People like Declan are, unfortunately, doing something. And unfortunately, that's all they can do.

Something.

XX.

We spent the day following a cat. I know that sounds strange, but let's be honest, we passed strange a long time ago. It had been a few weeks since the incident with Declan, the would-be arsonists, and the trees. Already, in the warming April sunshine, tribal lines were divvied up across the village. The hill sat strongly in cult territory, stretching down the Rye Hill and into Ryevale, where I met Shepard in his humble abode. The arsonists claimed everything else from the Salmon Leap, the "Lep", through Main Street, and up towards Louisa Bridge. This meant the cult had the front entrance to the park, and the arsonists had the back entrance. The park had become their new battlefield.

I wasn't invited again to more attempts to burn down the trees. Maybe they thought I was a jinx, or a sleeper agent for Shepard. Whatever the reason, I only heard about the subsequent attacks after the fact, either through idle gossip in the shops or the few times they were reported in the newspaper. Each attempt proved fruitless, though Declan was becoming something of a folk hero in the alt-right manosphere online. Couple that with Declan's deforming appearance, continuously suffering from fire burns to his skin, scarring him beyond recognition, and he was beginning to give Shepard competition in the whole crazy-evil-nobody category.

The next time I saw Declan, he was choking Shepard on the pitch by the trees. I was walking Diva, making the most of the sun in between light showers. The temperature was finally above ten. It was warm enough now for Diva to not need her coat. Even I myself had discarded my under-fleece, just going out with my jean jacket and paddy cap in case it rained. The scuff on my sunglasses I had to focus past was an unpleasant reminder I needed a new pair. We went through the front entrance to the park, now manned by cult members. The few remaining hold-outs (who hadn't died or left) were being pressured to join the cult in order to be allowed into the park, but I didn't get any sort of trouble. Instead, the worse I got was an acknowledging nod as I entered, most likely at Shepard's command. Maybe Declan was right; I mean, I wouldn't know I was a sleeper agent if I was one, would I?

Continuing on, I found the arsonists and the cult scrapping in that pitch, with the trees swaying and shaking, highly amused. The Mega-Tree in the centre was definitely bigger, and was definitely arcing forward. The fat pyramid I had seen before was elongated and stretching so far out its shadow was exceeding past the limits of the paddock walls. Was it just me or was it listing a little to the right, towards the sun?

As with before, the arsonists were overpowered by the surprisingly strong cult members, left fleeing for their lives, trying to pat out the flames accidentally catching onto them, or else screaming as they were tossed over the wall. Closest to the trench by the paddock walls was Declan, on top of Shepard, choking him with his grip, squeezing his neck. Shepard could only throw punch after punch at Declan's ears, wincing with each blow. We stood there, watching. The trees aren't benevolent. The trees aren't nefarious. They're just old gods, on par with how the wind or lightning used to be worshipped. I would say we've reverted back to our primitive forms... but have we ever left?

Diva began barking, pulling and running the length of her retractable lead. I looked down the footpath and saw, traipsing along merrily, a cat. It was a light grey Persian, trotting along, crossing the path and walking out onto the pitch. I followed it with my eyes, confused by its nonchalance.

There were man-eating trees enjoying a fight between the cult that worships them and the reactionaries who think they're funded by, I don't know, Bill Gates lets say, there's a tree growing so tall it looks like it could fall, and then there's this cat. Apparently I wasn't the only one interested in the cat, as the quarrel amongst the two groups simmered down to a quiet hush, all watching, panning slowly as the cat proudly pranced up the pitch, down the trench, leaped up onto the wall, and then over it, vanishing into the trees.

We all waited for several long minutes. Could the trees now consume animals? Could they attract pets? Would Shepard have to open up a farm to appease them now? No. Our stunned patience was rewarded with only more shock as, to everyone's surprise, further down from where we had seen it vanish, the cat sprang back up onto the wall, contently sitting briefly, licking its belly, before hopping down and trotting back across the pitch.

By this point, even Diva had stopped barking, following, as we all did, the cat, walking over the bulbous and misshapen pitch. One by one, the cult members and arsonists picked themselves up and began walking after the cat. I must admit, it intrigued me as well. I had no reason to follow, but I don't think anyone has any reason for much any more. You most certainly don't. So... we all followed the cat.

The cat swaggered up the main path parallel to the trees, turning left at the BMX track, across the now empty park ranger cabin, past the long since disregarded playground, and down a turn which overlooked a nearby field of rapeseed flowers; a mustard sea of rippling waves in the breeze. What was impressive was how the hundred or so people present still managed to stick to the path when they could have easily tracked and trampled over the blooming daffodil beds and the shaggy thickets of overgrown grass. Maybe we all figured it was best to follow the cat's lead exactly, with each beany step.

Myself and Diva made our way from the back of the group to the front, joining Shepard and Declan, who had put aside their fight to the death for a once off alliance to follow a cat. Up close, I could see both men had a toll taken upon them. Shepard was ageing rapidly, from stress, I imagine. His salt-and-pepper hair was becoming more salt than pepper, with what darkness was left travelling down to under his eyes, pooling into heavy sacks of tired bags, sitting just above his creeping stubble spreading out from his once well maintained beard, now a rough nest of patchy hair. Thick rings of soon to be bruising skin were forming around his neck. Declan was fairing no better. The burns and boils upon his body were so bad that he was practically mummified beneath a wrap of bandages soaked in lotions. What little skin was exposed was scarlet, leathery, and filling with puss.

My eyes returned to the feline ahead of us. I could make out a pink collar around its neck, with the tinkle of a metallic tag chiming with each step. It was clean, well fed, and groomed. I've never been much of a cat person, but even I could see the beauty in this one, as could its owners by the care they must be giving it. I couldn't decide if I was thankful or curious by the thought this cat was owned. I think in the moment, however, all of us were just more focused on where the cat was leading us.

How many people had we all seen vanish into the trees? How many people were driven mad? How had a village been brought to near destitution, yet this cat just leapt in and out, as easy as slinking through bushes? How? How could people just leave, never to be seen again, but this little cat could bop in and out, caring nothing for the middle-finger it had given all of us? I know it's dominionist, but it doesn't make sense! It's not fair! It's not! I've been living in fear for months now, and this thing just doesn't care? It's not right!

We tracked the cat all the way through the park, down the road, through the estates and alleyway, out onto Captain's Hill, and down into the Riverforest estates. It must have looked bizarre to the last remaining families hiding in their homes, peeking through gaps in the closed curtains, to see a procession led by a fluffy Persian. Even stranger to see us all turning into a cul-de-sac and follow the cat up to a front door of a house. It sat down in front of a distorted side porch window, staring into it. We all stopped, going between the cat and the window. About an hour later, though it was still bright outside, a hallway light flicked on and the rippling visage of a tall woman appeared, about to ascend the blocky shapes of stairs, stopping, spotting the cat. She goes to the door and opens it, allowing the purring cat in, rubbing against her leg. The woman was about to close the door until she double took, opening it wider, looking out, unnerved by the staring throng.

The growing evening air was still and sparsely interrupted by the chirp of birds, the distant roar of aeroplanes sailing off into the sky, and the ever present hush of cars shooting across the motorway in and out of Dublin.

The woman closed the door on us. We all looked at each other, wondering the same thing. Shepard went up to knock on the door first. A moment later, the woman answered. Shepard puffed out his chest.

Blessings upon you, sister! The trees are pleased by our meeting, for we have come for—-

She closed the door on us.

Declan stepped up, rapping on the door, knocking vigorously. She answered, though this time repulsed by his unpleasant appearance.

Hello, missus. We were wondering could we talk to you about your cat? We want to know...

Declan stammered. It only occurred to us all there and then what did it really matter if the cat could go in and out of the trees? It wasn't like the cat was going to tell us anything; it's a cat. All that seemed to matter was that it was something new, unusual, and, most importantly, more than anyone else had to understand what the trees were.

Declan, desperate to keep the conversation going, offered the woman fifty euros for the cat. She slammed the door in our faces. Shepard banged his heavily etched fists against the door, screaming through the letter flap that he'll offer two hundred euros.

Five hundred!

Six!

A grand!

Two!

It was like seeing a memory from another angle, as the horde from the opposing groups swarmed the outside of the house, banging as they had done when they surrounded me and Diva before. Some hopped over a fence to the back garden, presumably to bang on the back windows and doors. Either that or, if the woman had a carnivorous tree like so many had in their back gardens, those people have just rushed to their deaths, their screams masked by the mayhem ensuing outside.

Myself and Diva didn't linger long. What would have been the point? I barely had fifty euros that week to myself, never mind offering it to anyone else. There was nothing here for us. Though as we were leaving, I did find it interesting that the woman's car, parked in the drive to her house, had a parking pass for the Intellex Processing campus on the outskirts of the village. It didn't mean anything. I just thought it was interesting.

XXI.

It was dark on Easter Sunday. So dark I would have gone back to sleep had Diva not started barking, wanting to go out for a wee. I grumbled, swearing, getting dressed since I was sleeping in the nip with the warming nights, slipping into a pair of slip-ons and shuffling through the house and to the door. It was only when I opened the front door, with Diva shooting out, parading in a circle, and then piddling on the gravel, that I realised it was still as dark as night during the day. Street lamps still shone in the shadow of the great behemoth, spanning and stretching across the blue sky, eclipsing us in a paradoxical night. The houses were all abandoned as their doors hung open, the last remaining residents standing on the street, gawking up at the mass of fir reaching from horizon to horizon; from East to West. The rippling sea of branches shuddered and moved with a breath of a giant, threatening to give out from its own weight. There was no taper, no convergence nor vanishing point; you wouldn't be able to tell if it was one straight body or if it grew in diameter as it went. It was the Mega-Tree growing in the centre of the paddock.

The disconcerting estrangement filled the silence left by us standing outside our homes, as though we thought the stretching rings of sappy branches would reach down and sweep us up if we dared speak. Night shrouded everything, yet in the short framed glimpses of the sky we could see was an expanse of powder blue, nauseously discombobulating our sense of time and place, like fleeting seconds of not recognising your own reflection, skewed and prolonged enough to disturb and distress. Imagine the dysphoric lurch to tear off one's skin in the dire hope that it would appease someone and grant you a modicum of release; the paradoxical feeling that death or self-flagellation would restore life to tranquillity.

We all watched, our necks craning up, settling into pangs of pain, as a rippling shudder ran the length of the tree, shushing a rattle of branches and creaking with the strain of buckling bark. Following the wave of moss green on the shaded underbelly of the tree, you could see the most westernly length was noisier; prickly like static from distance and myopia. So it was distorting its shape as it went on. Was it to block the sun completely?

We waited for another shudder, as if the monstrous creature was awakening, but no more came from the Mega-Tree. Instead, with a chorus of gnarling creaks, crashing glass, a percussion of cracking brick, and the horrified screams of women and men, the trees from the back gardens of our houses began to stretch upwards and grow. Willows, birches, oaks, aspens; they all ascended, scaling on a single axis, as if mocking us with just how horrendously misshapen and malformed they can make themselves. I turned to my roof and sure enough, I saw that the tree in our back was wriggling and worming its way up into the sky. It reminded me of those spores that infect an insect, eat their insides, and then sprout a nimbly stem that bursts and spews more spores, repeating the process. Are we insects?

Up, up, and up they went, carrying with them pieces of houses and the garden. There was a skinny aspen that sprinkled dust and crumbling nuggets of cinder-blocks after most likely breaking through a wall. The willow in Mary's back looked clumsy with the tarp still shrouding it, blowing off and drifting down into the next estate once it was high enough. We all watched, mortified, as an elm, broad and bulbous, carried away a bed, with a single, sleeping arm hanging over the side. I hope for their sake they're dead. Each one of the trees, stretching up hundreds of metres into the sky, vanished into the shadowy chasms in between the bushy branches, giving the almost comical appearance of a spindle legged shaggy centipede.

How long we stood there, anticipating something else miraculously hellish to appear next, I couldn't say for sure, but at some point that nosey Emma Murphy from three doors down brought out her old portable FM radio and yelled for everyone to listen. The radio was so small and far away that ironically our reaction was to noisily rush over to hear better. Diva gained the ire of Emma as she snorted and grunted along after me as I jogged over.

Once we all settled, we could hear an RTÉ news report confirm that it wasn't just our imagination; there was indeed a giant tree in the sky. Thank God; I was starting to worry. Aerial imagery was able to show, according to the report, that the tree was originating from the paddock and was landing and seemingly burrowing into Maynooth. I wondered if it was the business park. One of the local drug dealers in the estate chortled and announced how it wasn't any loss; it was only Maynooth. The shush and disdainful glances quickly silenced them. The news reporter, I think it was Eoin or Ian or something, fell silent as well, as though he heard us, but the rush of steps and rustle of papers from a station producer hinted that instead breaking news had just been received. The mumbling and heated whispers between the two drew us in closer with hungry curiosity and a fattening desire for information. Finally, a roar erupted, repelling everyone from the radio like a shock-wave.

I'VE GOT FAMILY THERE!

The producer, hissing and rushing incoherently in a hushed tone filled with stinging harshness, was able to at least contain themselves enough to pull us back in, straining to make out their words, echoing them out loud in part to confirm with each other we had heard them right.

Do it?

I don't care?

Good as dead?

Do your job?

Spreading?

Finally, Eoin or Ian or something returned, unable to contain the emotion and the struggle to not cry from appearing in every punch of every syllable. The government had been monitoring the situation in Leixlip closely and have come to the decision that military force is necessary to combat the Mega-Tree. As such, they've sought aid from the government and air-force of the United Kingdom, who have confirmed that they will be sending fighter jets to intercept it. In a quivering pause, the reporter clarified that the RAF are going to fire missiles at the Mega-Tree and as such all remaining residents of Leixlip are to stay inside and seek shelter as best as we could.

Leixlip being Leixlip, of course nobody listened. We all stood there, waiting to see if we would survive. Or maybe we hoped that if we were to die there and then, at least there was going to be a show.

XXII.

We were all waiting to die when Sibhann Sullivan came out with trays of teas, biscuits, and chocolates. She apologised; they were unopened from Christmas, which was only a problem for the old biddies recoiling in dismay. I took a Twirl and a chocolate digestive because of Sibhann's goading. Eric Sullivan, her closeted husband, was hurrying out with more cups when I earned a raised eyebrow from Sibhann by saying I took my tea black and without sugar.

Those of us who were whiling away the time watched others panic packing whatever they could rush into suitcases and into their cars, driving off. Some forgot the kids, leaving them crying at the door. Most didn't turn back for them. They were unlikely to get far. Though interest in the trees had waned somewhat to the outside world, an unofficial stance was taken that we were to be isolated as much as possible to Leixlip. Fewer buses and trains ran through the village these days. Those of us who commuted for work were made to Work-From-Home, or else were let go entirely out of the blue, as though what was happening here was contagious. Given the news about the airstrike, we speculated the roads were bound to be blocked off. To everyone outside of Leixlip, we were as much the problem as the trees. After all, people in Lucan don't have killer trees, so it must be something we're doing, right?

I was eavesdropping on the gossip between Hannah Kyteler and Fran Reilly about Cathleen Bailey having it off with Adam MacDiarmid shortly before Declan arrived.

So then, you know what she says to me!

Go on love, what did she say?

She says, listen to this, have you ever heard this, she says what I do and don't do with whoever is none of your business, Mrs. Fran Reilly, so I'll thank you to find someone else's life to vicariously live through!

She did not!

She did!

The cheeky cow!

Oh, she's fierce for mickey, that one, so she is! Mad for it! Froths at the mouth! Always has.

No surprised there. Just look at her mother.

No!

Aye!

A banged up, matte silver, mid-two-thousands Toyota chortled and rattled up the road into the estate, screeching as it took the hard turn, scattering a few residents as they leapt out of its way. Declan, puffing with rushing breaths, climbed out of the car with some difficulty, rushing up to me, asking demandingly what have I been doing.

I was sitting on the wall in front of my house with Diva beside me, attempting to sneak the chocolate digestive biscuit from my grip. Everyone in the estate was now staring at us; an eerie, anxiety inducing feeling only further heightened by the darkness enshrouding us all. I turned back to Declan, who, somehow, was looking even worse than before. What little skin was previously exposed was completely covered with more bandages. His hair, formerly left to sit upon his crown like an animal's pelt, was nowhere to be seen. His right leg was encased in an orthopaedic boot; thick, black, and, going by Declan's throwing stride, heavy. But none of this was what caught my attention the most.

I used my nibbled biscuit to point and ask what happened to his left hand, which was missing.

Oh! That! Yeah... don't worry about that! Now come on!

Declan went to pull me into the car, spilling my tea and dropping the biscuit. I yanked myself from Declan's grip, picked up Diva, who swore at me for grabbing her just before she could chow down on the biscuit, and rushed her back into the house, despite her barks of protest. I returned to Declan, asking what was he in such a hurry for. Again, he huffed and puffed, aghast and flustered, as though I was the reason he was late for some important appointment. At last, he just pointed up at the sky... or at least where there would be sky if not for the hulking tree spanning overhead. I followed his finger as he gave out, shouting and swearing about this being our chance to burn the Mega-Tree, and stared up at the tree, drowning out Declan's insane rambling, hoping he'd get the message that I wasn't interested in going with him. I told him as much when I asked what did he need me for. He started and stopped several times, searching desperately for something to use against me and carry me off in a gust of aspirational conviction. What he managed was a little more pitiful.

You're the Tree Guy! That has to mean something! It has to mean something! It has to!

I stared at him. A man with his skin flayed away, one limb broken, another missing. That's where his meaning had gotten him; a slow cooked human. But it did occur to me that he was on to something. Surely a target as big as the heavens would be easier to set alight than before. What was the cult going to do? Stop us in hot-air balloons? And if we could set the Mega-Tree on fire, perhaps it would stop the jet fighters before they arrived. We just needed to get high enough. But how?

Jumping into the car with Declan, which was littered with cigarette butts and crumpled cans of cheap cider, stinking of smoke, pus, and the dying gasps of a discoloured car air-freshener, I was surprised once down the hill that he took a left towards the Salmon Leap and not right towards Maynooth. Another turn and a five minutes drive later, and we were pulling into the nearby Weston Airport. You'd often see the planes, usually small seaters, often for recreational flyers. We drove up the road to the car park, circling the main building. Though it was quiet, we could just make out the darkened silhouettes of staff in the control tower. Declan didn't slow down as we came into the car park. On the contrary, he sped up, driving into and breaking through the metal fencing.

Declan knew better than to slow down and instead sped up, skidding and leaving marks as he took a hard left, heading for a small grouping of light aircraft left in the open, either on display or awaiting use that day. Declan screeched to a halt and again struggled to get out of the car. I rushed over to his side, looking up at the control tower, just making out figures frantically pointing at us and banging on the windows before vanishing from view. I tried to hurry Declan along.

THE BOOT! THE BOOT!

I mistook Declan for a moment as I thought he wanted me to pull him out by his orthopaedic boot first, but when he repeated himself, angrier this time, I realised he meant the car boot. I open it and found a sloshing pile of molotovs, seeping in their own leaking juices, either cracked or loosened from the bumpy ride. I grabbed as many as were still in good enough condition, cradling a dozen, following the hobbling Declan to an untethered plane; a Cessna Seventeen-Two-A. Something suddenly struck me. I asked Declan, just before he ducked under the wing and punched his heavily bandaged fist through the window, where were the other members of the arsonist group.

Oh? Well... Either the trees got them or the woke mob did. You know who I blame?

It's that time again! Let's play everyone's favourite game; Guess The Reactionary Bullshit! Thirty seconds to answer correctly. Is it, A, Feminists, B, Foreigners, C, The EU, or D, George Soros? Input your answers now!

Both thankfully and unfortunately Declan didn't keep me in bated breath.

The Feminists! All my friends told me their wives told them to stop coming to the meetings. They used feminism against them.

To this day I still don't know what he meant by "using feminism against them". I asked about the boy, the one he sent into the shit farm. I didn't have long to mull over his silence as Declan climbed in through the broken window and kicked open the door for me, just as the staff and security finally made their way out. I tossed the bottles of murky whiskey and unsettlingly yellow vodka into the back behind our seats, just as Declan started the engine and propellers, erupting into a hellish cry of shrieking, deafening noise. We both looked around, searching the roof above us, but there were no noise mufflers. There was no time to worry about our loss of hearing, as security was closing in on us. Declan pushed down on the accelerator and we crawled forward, picking up enough to evade the security struggling not to collapse from exhaustion behind us. We followed a track onto the runway, picking up enough speed for the force to press us back into our seats before pulling back the steering wheel and slowly rise into the air, heading for the crevice of light in the distance.

It was strange, coming back into the light of the afternoon as easily as one steps out into a rain shower from under a shelter. Suddenly, but completely. Once we were far enough out of the shadow cast by the Mega-Tree, the sun flooded and drown us instantaneously. Declan, flinching to shield his eyes, dipped the plane a little. My stomach lurched in the free-fall so badly it took a little while before I felt okay enough to look out through the window. It really was a gorgeous day. The unencumbered sun shone down on the stretches of green and the speckled spots of towns and villages littering the land. Ghostly wisps of grey blurs brushed past, bringing a further chill into the plane through the broken window, but it did little to ruin the jigsaw puzzle of fields and homes revealing itself to us. Looking up to the horizon gave the impression of a haze bleeding into the pastel blue sky, with only the most miniscule interruption by distant planes descending into Dublin or a pillowy puff of cloud wandering off towards Westmeath. I would have happily forgotten what we were up here for if it wasn't for Declan listing us to the left, turning a full one-eighty, bringing the Mega-Tree back into focus.

With the distance and height, I could now see the Mega-Tree wasn't as arched as it appeared on the ground, but rather had the shape more aligned with an unbent staple; up relatively straight from the paddock, shooting across the village in a straight line, and then vertically plunging into Maynooth. Judging by how the motorway to my right appeared to be going underneath it, the same motorway I had to cross to get to the Job-Way meetings, I knew for certain the Mega-Tree was burrowing into the business park.

The surrounding growl of the engine, the translucent, whirling blur of the propellers, and the frigid whistle of the elevated wind pouring through the broken window meant myself and Declan had to shout as loudly as possible to even come close to being heard.

WE'LL GET OVER IT AND YOU DROP THE MOLOTOVS! I THINK IF I STRAFE TO THE LEFT WE CAN RUN UP ITS BACK OR WHATEVER AND SPREAD THE FIRE! HOLD ON! WE'LL NEED TO GET CLOSE SO THE MOLOTOVS AREN'T SUFFOCATED ON THE WAY DOWN!

Closer and closer we got, descending slowly. I think Declan was experiencing the same sensation of spooks as I was because, as the Mega-Tree grew ahead of us, I could see his throat flex with sharp inhales before dipping the plane up slightly. Perhaps he was fighting his own urge to flee. I think this has to be one of the few cases where someone literally has a flight-or-fight response to danger.

With the unencumbered sunlight hitting the topside of the Mega-Tree, coupled with the closer look at what we were dealing with, we made out the branches were still rippling in melodic rhythm, just nowhere near as pronounced as the shudder the estate had witnessed earlier. Stranger still, the billowing waves were interrupted by the odd flick, whip, and coiling of tips, like green tentacles searching for prey to crack open and tear apart. Amidst this sea of thick overgrowth, floundering desperately to survive, came the wild pleading hands and wide-eyed calls for help. It was the man from the bed that was raised up and carried away by one of the trees. I called to Declan, going hoarse with the yells needed to overcome the noise in the plane, that we needed to get lower and skim over the surface to try rescuing them.

WHAT COLOUR IS HE!

Oh for Christ's sake!

Before I could admonish him, there was a whooshing gust streaking past us, shunting the plane aside with the force of the slipstream. Another on the opposite side rattled us so violently Declan lost control of the wheel with his remaining hand. I grabbed hold of it to level us out and stop us from listing further to one side. The two light aircraft planes ahead of us were joined by a third that came out from under us. As one turned on its wing, we caught a glimpse of some recognisable faces; members of Shepard's cult. And with them turning around, heading straight for us, just short of clipping our wings as I dipped out of the way, it was clear they were here to stop us. So much for hot air-balloons.

There was nowhere to run or hide; I don't think you can get any more exposed than the sky on a clear day. Declan managed to regain his composure and grabbed the wheel again. Ahead of us, the third plane coming out from under us levelled out with the door opening on the left side. I leaned forward, squinting, desperately trying to focus on the hands stretching out from the co-pilot seat, busy at work on the hinges of the door with what looked like a power drill. Once I saw the top bolt zip past us in the air, I grabbed hold of the wheel from Declan and pressed forward, diving the plane out of the way of the door, finally unlatched, careening in the air, though it did still strike and tumble across our roof. Declan was too busy swearing at me to fully appreciate I had narrowly saved us from losing our left wing.

Declan corrected our flight path as we reached the mass of the Mega-Tree, tantalisingly close to brushing the licking tongue-like branches, working laboriously hard to try and savour the taste of rubber and metal just out of its reach.

DROP THE MOLOTOVS!

I screamed back about the man still clambering to stay afloat in the bramble. He was a squirming speck at this distance, but with the speed we were going we would have less than a minute to decide what we were doing.

HOW DO WE KNOW HE'S NOT TRYING TO TRICK US!

How! How and why would someone risk their own life to be rescued, randomly, by a plane it didn't even know would be flying past? I tried explaining I had seen this man get swept up by the trees as they grew from our gardens. If we didn't save him, he was either going to be swallowed up by the Mega-Tree, burned alive by the molotovs, or else obliterated once the jet fighter got here.

Declan went silent. For a brief moment, I had the fleeting hope that finally I had gotten through to Declan. That was until he had another go.

MIGRANTS!

...What!

MIGRANTS! THAT'S WHY! THEY SNEAK IN, DON'T THEY! FIRST THEY PRETENDED TO BE ASYLUM SEEKERS, THEN THEY TRIED GETTING HERE ON BOATS, NOW THEY'RE USING THE TREES! WE SAVE ONE AND WE'LL HAVE A THOUSAND NEXT WEEK! IT'S ALL PART OF THE LEFTIST AGENDA TO DEPOPULATE US AND—-

Shut up! Shut up! Shut the fuck up, you thick, stupid cunt!

Declan fell silent, stunned. So stunned, he paid little attention to the cult member who had just jumped out of a passing plane overhead, landing on top of us, lost their grip, and fell off, vanishing into the Mega-Tree with a muffled scream. I just kept going. I kept at him. Did he hear how all this sounded? How much word-salad he was tossing about without the faintest idea of what he was saying? Why! Why would there be a conspiracy for every little thing? How can someone see people just as scared, lost, and terrified as them, but instead of wanting to help they just listen to made up bullshit! People are dying and you're crying about people you don't like? Why! Why are you willing to isolate yourself from people because of your fears? Why!

Declan, still silent, looked out to the front of the plane, but I could see how unfocused he was. He didn't even react when one of the cult's planes nosedived straight into the Mega-Tree, swallowed up as easily as if it fell into water. The thin, chapped and sickly smoothed lips tucked in. I looked out ahead as well, but likewise, I wasn't really paying attention. I was sitting with him, waiting for him to parse his hurt feelings.

I have to be right.

The engine was still roaring, and the wind was still whistling, yet I heard him as clear as if both had abruptly disappeared. Maybe our ears had adjusted, or I could guess from context how to read his lips, but I sat there, letting him speak.

I have to be right. I have to be... because otherwise it means I don't know what's going on. So I have to be right... right?

I disliked Declan strongly. I'm sure if I had been more hostile and dismissive upon our first meeting, he would have quickly distanced himself from me. But for those brief seconds, before he opened his door and threw himself out, dropping down and vanishing into the Mega-Tree with the battle cry "give me back my hand you bastard", I felt a twinge of pity. It didn't absolve him, no more than it would anyone else, but it was at least reassuring to see that the fear we were all experiencing was shared by the arrogantly confident. It's just such a shame that those with tenacity are so often terrified to the point of self-harm and lashing out. I'm sorry you were scared, Declan. It's a shame you couldn't see we all were too.

BANG!

The plane rattled and shook, scooping me back from my melancholic malaise, grabbing hold of the wheel, I jumped into Declan's former seat, pulling up slightly. I couldn't see the man anywhere ahead of us, and the plane moved with a delayed heft; I think he must have grabbed on to the joint between the two wheels. Once again, another body smacked into the plane from above, this time rolling onto the nose and getting caught up in the propellers, hurled around for a few rotations before getting fired off over the side of the Mega-Tree, shrinking on the way down. Morbidly leaning over to watch, I caught sight of three glints in the distance, growing in size quickly. It was the RAF.

Listing to the right, I kept my eyes on the growing dots of shimmering silver, gradually stretching out into pin thin widths as their wing span came into focus. Eerily, besides the thunderous rumble of the engine, the sky was uninterrupted by the jets approaching, travelling far ahead of their own broken sound barriers. It was strange to behold. I mean... it was, until I noticed, from the corner of my eyes, to my left, the Mega-Tree once again pulsating, shivering along its length. Then, contracting first, as though inhaling, the Mega-Tree shot out a thick, stretching branch, worming and slithering in the air as easily as an eel in water, racing for the rapidly approaching jets. It listed widely to the West, seemingly missing the jets, but with ungodly strength and swiftness, the bushy tentacles, casting a slithering shadow across much of Leinster, swatted the jets and vaporised them in a puff of explosive debris and smoke. The tip snatched and coiled around a collection of falling wreckage and retracted back into the Mega-Tree with such speed I can never be sure if I did or didn't see the pilots desperately trying to free themselves. I tell myself some nights it was a trick of the light. Either way, so much for the RAF.

You may be surprised to hear this... but I don't know how to fly a plane. Yes, the basic steering is the same as a car, just with the added features of going up and down, but the rest of the intimidating buttons, dials, and levers in front of me might as well be for a quantum computer. I could turn and go up and down. That was it. Even if I could land, it's not like I could go back to Weston and risk arrest. And then there was the issue of our friend on the wheels, if he was still there. I couldn't keep flying indefinitely either, though I was beginning to develop an appreciation for the vast freedom of the skies. My only option was to jump and hope for a soft landing.

With no clue if my friend was dead a couple hundred meters below, I bellowed out the broken window for someone to hold on. We descended over the side of the Mega-Tree, churning its branches as though chewing. Once low enough, I leaned over to the left and spotted Maynooth station, a short way from the end of the Mega-Tree burrowing back into the Earth. Strafing over the tracks, I followed the canal, returning into the colossal shadow. It was like stepping through a waterfall; a heavy curtain of force that suddenly weigh down upon you punishingly. A few times, I had to pick up as we dipped further still, much to the whine of the engine. The propellers were starting to slow, damaged from the body falling into it. We were just feet above the surface of the canal when we got to Louisa Bridge. The Hill would be the next stop, but at this height, and with no give from the plane as I tried gaining air, this seemed as good a place to bail as any.

I listed the plane to the right, turning the last corner before Confey Bridge, an old stone convex archway crossing the canal, unfortunately at the same height as our trajectory. It was either jump or crash. I climbed out of my seat and kicked open the door, struggling to keep it open with the speed we were going at. Climbing out, holding onto a stabilising beam for the wing and the door, I looked down and saw the man, still holding on to the joint for the wheels, latching on like a baby animal. The poor man was shivering in his underwear. His eyes caught mine.

Outside, the plane was a little more bearable when it came to hearing myself shout for him to jump. Anguished, his teeth bared in a feeble grimace, he shook his head and shouted back an unintelligible string of words probably amounting to a simple no. I repeated myself, this time pointing at the canal. No doubt it would be frigid, even in Spring, and a jump at this speed was bound to be ungraceful and disorientating, but the bank was right there. Again, he cowered, huddling back into himself, hiding his face behind the beam. I sat back in the chair, still holding the door open with my foot, leaned back and stretched for one of the molotovs. I stood back up, and looked back at the man.

HEY!

The man looked back at me, and I gave him no warning as I skulled him in the face with the butt of the bottle I fired, sending him rolling into the canal. I had wasted too much time. Maybe I knew that when I turned around, looking ahead of the plane, and found the stonework engulfing my view. It's a little muddled what exactly happened next, but there were flashing streaks of light and darkness, a chorus of shattering, scraping, crumpling, and splashing, followed by numbing, pulsating thumps, sharp, stabbing cold, and consuming, smothering, water. I can't remember everything, but I can remember the blackness; the closest to death I've ever been.

XXIII.

I awoke, however much later, on the stripped, hardwood floor of an empty yet not unused bedroom. The pain in my chest stirred me, catching in my throat, like upcoming bile, stinging and hissing, lingering on my tongue the unpleasant taste of dirt and waste from years of decaying reeds, fish, and the occasionally discarded used condom. I couldn't settle on whether to vomit or swallow, not knowing which would be more relief. A fist thumped to the chest was enough to burst the swelling bubble of bile steaming the stench to the back of my nostrils.

A few welcomed gulps of air strengthened me into a sitting position, supported by my hands pressing down upon the textured grain of the wood. My eyes adjusted to the darkness; a door left ajar allowed for some light to seep in. The odd items of half drunk bottles of Fanta, tattered and dog-eared books, grease stained travel pillows, and balls of clothes showed some sign of life, but there was no bed, blankets, or anything that gave the impression people weren't sleeping on the floor.

Pushing myself up and onto my feet, I looked outside the curtainless window. I wouldn't have thought it possible; it was darker than before. From the distant horizon of sky just visible beyond the Mega-Tree, a subtle difference could be noticed; a more Byzantium shade defined the edges, meeting the harsher, hungrier black. I must have been out cold all day. I went for my pocket, discovering my phone was taken off me. I had no way of knowing how late it was. I took one last searching glance around the room before leaving.

The upstairs landing, stairs, and hall were just as bare. Lone staples and wispy threads from edges on the same hardwood floorboards left hints that a carpet had roughly been torn and pulled up in a hurry, for whatever reason. My steps rang out with reverberating knocks so pronounced I had to stop, wincing in the silence, but when a faint whisper from downstairs didn't stop, I thought there was no point in creeping, continuing to announce my approach with each ringing tap. It was only when I got down to the front hall that I recognised the house; it was Shepard's.

The whispering grew clearer, wafting out from the front room. From the bottom step I could just make out Shepard's back, standing at the furthest point from the door. I couldn't make him out fully, nor exactly what he was saying. Maybe had I left there and then, I could have stopped them from taking Diva. In hindsight, I think they were counting on me getting distracted. My curiosity got the better of me. I went into the front room, standing back to listen.

What does it mean? Tell me! I've done everything for you! I've fed you. I've indulged you. I've protected you. Answer me. I have done everything. You can't deny me any longer! What does it mean?

Shepard stood right in front of the window, looking up at the Mega-Tree's underside, his hands clasped together just beneath his quivering lips. His reflection in the glass was gaunt and sickly; exhaustion, stress, and paranoia was finally eating away at his drying, crackling skin, eroding his face. What was once a handsome, almost fatherly, good looking man was now a dishevelled mess, steaming with a putrid stink of sweat and smoke. He was about to continue when his eyes shot off to his side, meeting mine in his reflection.

There was no performance of comradery nor intimidation like all other times. His eyes lingered heavily upon me, a mixture of remorse and contempt, as though he was sorry I had forced him to do something. His cheeks were pinned up in a solemn smile, like he wanted me to not worry, knowing I would soon react badly. I called out to him when he made no movement, making sure he wasn't lost in his thoughts again.

Hello, Witness.

He turned around to face me. In the light, his thin, waxy skin was softer than his reflection made it appear in the shadows, but was nonetheless unhealthy and disturbing. It's like seeing a movie star go to seed mercilessly quickly, fixating on every tiny ageing wrinkle decrying lost youth. He was slow, tired, and disappointedly disinterested, like I was a chore, something that had to be dealt with.

I'm glad you've come back to us... someone is looking out for you.

When I asked what happened, he reached into his pocket and checked his phone, putting it away before sighing, forcing a placating smile.

Some of my flock spotted your wreckage from their own plane. We'll discuss what you were doing with that Declan fellow another time. That reminds me; I should send an apology to Weston Airport for commandeering their planes as well. As I was saying, they pulled you out of the water, but you were knocked out from the impact. You were brought here. There was no point trying to call for an ambulance. In the ensuing panic, they've been preoccupied. All this talk of the RAF and giant trees; it's no wonder people think this is the end.

The last few sentences went over my head a little, as I couldn't help noticing we were alone. Shepard must have guessed I was getting suspicious because he was quick to continue.

I was worried. When they brought you here, I mean. I offered to stay and wait to see if you recovered. Would you like a drink? Or maybe something to eat? You must be hungry.

I tried listening over Shepard, concentrating hard to pick up anything other than his droning pleasantries. The only thing that silenced him was asking where was everyone. A sharp inhale was cut short by the flicker of a smile dropping into a pensive stare; blank and flat. There was an internal debate going on inside Shepard, of how little to say to appease me. Finally, he settled on what he must have thought was consolingly detached stoicism.

You're not like us. You never were. I can see that now. I think I knew from the beginning. You hesitate. You pause before you speak. And I know why. You're scared. You're panicking. That little racing feeling in your chest, that voice that screams to run, that primal urge to do anything it takes to make the looming uncertainty of the monstrously apathetic vanish. That is what drives you. No matter how irrational it seemed, how out of character, how stupid, it was that will to live, your will to live that made you stop, made you name the park ranger, made you examine that twig, made you join in on the arson attacks and follow that cat. That is why you've stayed. You're scared. In the face of insurmountable horrors, we do whatever we can, even if it doesn't make sense. Especially if it doesn't make sense, because what good is logic against the incomprehensible? Madness is self-preservation brought to its end. The problem isn't that we've lost our minds. The problem, my dear Witness, it that you haven't joined us. Like you, I'm trying everything. Even if it doesn't make sense, because what's the harm? Nothing else makes sense. So... I am sorry... but I have to try everything to contain and appease the trees... Everything and anything... including your dog.

A sickening chill surging in my veins was numbed by the thumping heat of Shepard's breath and body pressing against and stopping me from escaping, holding me against the wall. Up close, I could see his teeth were stained in blood from inflamed gums; he spoke with the stink of a chain-smoker.

Nothing is working! Bombs, bullets, prayers! There must be something to stop the trees, to control them, to keep them under our dominion. There must be something; there has to be! We aren't going to find out if we don't keep trying! We must try everything! And yes, that means your dog! We can't let it end like this! Not for one stupid animal!

I tucked up my legs, pinned up by Shepard, and kicked off his chest, dropping to the floor with a painful thud, but in that moment adrenaline hurried me out of the house. Tearing down the dark road, passing the whistling, abandoned homes, I only glanced over my shoulder as I heard the squeal of car breaks, still puttering as it stopped outside Shepard's house. I saw the hunched and presumably winded

Shepard get escorted into the back of the car. I didn't care to wonder where they were going, hurrying down the steep decline, crossing the bridge over the Rye river, gushing fat, foaming tumbles of water, sprinting past the long dead nursing home, puffing up the steep hill leading to my estate.

The crowd of neighbours was gone, having grown bored with waiting to die. No one saw me shoulder slam my own front door open, too distraught to realise I had my keys with me. Stumbling, my limbs thrown wildly, my eyes ricocheting in every direction, I called out for Diva. She wasn't in the front room, the toilets, nor the bedroom. My relief that the back door, still shrouded by the bushy willow in the garden, remained closed was short-lived as I heard from behind me the rustle of steps and breathing.

Entering the kitchen, followed by three men, was the sneering, aged pout of Tabitha, proudly folding her arms and smiling as I came back, searching between the four of them for an explanation. Tabitha obliged; Diva was taken to be prepared for the sacrifice. They knew I'd come here first if I thought she hadn't been taken yet. We were all to wait here, Tabitha went on, like good little boys and girls, as she put it, until it was complete. I had other ideas.

A kitchen was a very poor choice for a stand-off, especially after threatening to kill my dog. I really don't know how they thought this was going to go down, but I doubted, as I reached into a creaking cupboard, pulling out a small pot, that they were prepared for me to put up a fight.

The gong of the flat, blackened pot bottom rang out as it cracked across and twisted the face of one of the men, sending him falling to the side, smacking his head off the edge of the counter, oozing out blood in cascading sheets of rose, caking his face as he held it in anguish. A second man, bravely stepping forth to take Tabitha's spot as she backed off, got the pot tossed into his face, breaking and compressing his nose, blinding him with the numbing, hot throb in the centre of his skull, sputtering either from shock, broken pieces of nasal bone, or, with any luck, both getting caught in his throat. The third man lunged for me, but wasn't quick enough to straighten up in time to avoid me, jumping out of the way and snatching a sharp cooking knife from the magnetic rack, stabbing him in his side.

With the howl of pain and paralysing shock distracting him, I pulled out the crimson imbibing blade and plunged it back in again, this time catching him in the heart, spurting out a squirt like zest hissing from fruit. I kept going, in and out, for however long it took Tabitha to finally step forward and toss me off the man, who fell slump onto the floor, the light in his eyes dimming in the encroaching abyss.

The impact against the door loosened my grip on the knife, clattering on the tiled floor next to the first man, still screaming and slipping in his own wet puddle of juices. I spun around and had the door open, nearly escaping, before Tabitha's wide, ragged hands pressed down upon me, a sudden weight falling straight onto my shoulders, tossing me back across the kitchen. She stamped over to me, her arms hulking on either side. I threw a punch, and she took it like a champ, grabbing my wrist for support, pulling me to one side, nearly tripping. In the time it took me to turn around, Tabitha had raced over and head-butted me with such forced I finally went down, shielding my forehead with my palm, momentarily forgetting where I was. I narrowly picked myself up into a sitting position in time to avoid Tabitha's slamming stomp where my pelvis formerly was, sending her reeling back, damaging her own ankle.

I rolled over to my right, scrambled to my feet, and head to the back door. I had no plan, but the fear surging through my body was clouding my judgement. I didn't get a chance to damn my stupidity, cornering myself in a dead end, because, when I turned around, five burly fingers sunk themselves into my supple neck; prey for Tabitha to immobilise. My desperate fingers, struggling against Tabitha's strength, were useless when it came to stopping the repeated punches to the face

I received, each either loosening a tooth, swelling an eye, fracturing a cheek bone, or else shoving my head back into the window of the back door, feeding the crack in it. I was either going to be choked or bludgeoned to death. Only for the squirrelly strength to duck out of the way of another punch, letting Tabitha's fist break through the window, I'd be dead.

Lower down on the ground, I looked up, still cornered by Tabitha's body, hearing a sharp, shallow gasp coupled with widening eyes, I felt a twinge of remorse. Tabitha looked down, her hand still sticking out through the broken window, her eyes meeting mine with a stinging anger, like it was my fault we were all damned.

With a clatter of glass and breaking bones, Tabitha was sucked out through the door in a blink, as though through a pinhole rupture in outer space, swallowed up by the indifferently hungry, surrounding blackness. Shock, thankfully, didn't paralyse me, affording me the head start needed to narrowly escape the cancerous growth of willow branches and roots slapping and slinging onto every surface it landed on through the gaping hole, spreading infectiously. Its bark scabbed and hardened like leathery rot, continuing to spread and grow as a tsunami would across a seaside village.

Throwing myself back into the back hall, slamming my side into a door, I could see, for the second I wasted, the latching mesh of webbing tendrils was seeping into the house after me, not just claiming the walls, ceiling, and floor but shooting out threads of matter into the open air, landing with spanning splatters, only further engulfing more of the house. It was these same infecting threads, connecting to one another like a network of festering veins, I had to jump over to escape into the kitchen, finding two of the injured men desperately trying to aid each other with fistfuls of dampened, mahogany red soaked tea towels. The third man lay dead. In the time, mere nanoseconds, it took to reach the door, the willow tree had swallowed the hall, tearing it off the house like succulent meat off a carcass, stretching into the kitchen and pulling the corpse into itself, golloping it up savagely. The two men, finally realising the danger they were in, went to join me but were too late.

Closing the door behind me on them, I gripped and pulled up the handle, securing the bolt in the latch, jumping up, and landing my feet against the frame. I was a one-man lock, using my own weight and muscles to keep the frantic and deranged screaming on the other side from escaping. It was ten long seconds of screams, calls for help, thunderous banging on the door, and the squelching, twisting, almost whip-like whooshes of branches wrapping around throats and crawling into strangled airways.

Then... silence.

An uneasy calm dropped upon me, so heavy I fell to the ground with comedic irony. I waited, almost hoping for the roots to come out through the walls and floorboards, but there was nothing. Just me. The smart thing to have done would have been to leave. But I, you know, like an eejit, was curious. I stood up, leaned forward, pressed my ear against the door, and waited.

I could hear nothing.

The door exploded, torn off its hinges, exposing a wriggling, slithering wall of organic matter, like a huge breeding ball of earthy serpents, taking up the whole volume of the kitchen, with whining creaks threatening to tear up the foundations. I stumbled back from this monstrous, abominable hellscape as it phased through the front hall with effortless ease. I shot for the front door, not bothering to close the porch door behind me. I leapt from the porch step and tumbled onto the gritted tarmac, rolling and turning to see the vines sprawl and grip onto the outside of the house, cracking and crushing it into a crumbling ruin, burying the tendrils beneath the rubble, dusting myself and a small radius around the house.

I stood up, coughing, trying to see through tearful eyes the striking emptiness that had been mine, Diva's, and my late partner's home. Gone. Forever.

I'm sorry. I'm sorry I've lost another piece of you. But I won't lose the last piece. Not to those trees.

I headed off, running down the road where Diva would bark proudly announcing to others she was on a walk, over the grassy hill where Diva would prance and gambol, through a stone walled path where I would often have to pull Diva from eating nettles, and racing out to an estate leading to St. Catherine's park where I'd often have to pull Diva from leaping onto the road from over-excitement. It was a path I could have crossed a million times before, yet now it felt as though I was racing through memories, poignant for how limited they now seemed, suddenly rare by the realisation of how finite life is. I won't let them do this; I won't let them take her. Not my Diva.

I cut across the pitch immediately inside the park as directly as I could. If I could have flown through the old monastery, briefly joining the ghosts haunting the grounds, I would have. But I had to suffer the agonising sprint past wilting flowers, starving for sunlight. If it wasn't for the ominous amber glow ahead, pulsating around the turn, I would have been lost in the darkness. I turned around the corner to the pitch and they were there.

Everyone.

The entire village of Leixlip.

It was a sea of sweltering fire. Candles, lanterns, lit furniture legs. Hundreds, maybe just shy of thousands, of the remaining residents were present, sweating in the collective heat, each highlighted and silhouetted in the living haze. They took up the length of the pitch, with many forced to stand as far back as the parallel path or in the neighbouring, fenced-off dog park. The aura of fire was able to reach the underbelly of the Mega-Tree, etching soft lines that could have been mistaken for bemused grins of pagan gods, leering down upon us disgusting, hopeless cretins; an infestation in their paradise. And leading them, Shepard.

He stood, elevated above the masses, on top of an unfolded ladder, once again needing the prophet on the mound effect to carry his voice and give him a legitimacy he never deserved. Over the flutter of flames and crackling torches, he spoke with the same deranged and unhinged fervour he desperately wanted to pull off.

My flock! You have seen the righteous anger and might the trees are capable of! Technology and weaponry are no match! Under their providence, we are sheltered, protected, and whittled down to you, those who have been mercifully spared, worthy of their love! But we must offer that love in return! And love is, if nothing else, an act of sacrifice! I give you our sacrifice!

Shepard was handed and held up Diva, shivering and crying out a high, heartbreaking whine. I couldn't help myself; I was incensed. I raced forward, forcing my way into the army. I only made it a few yards in before I was recognised; a murmur of acknowledgement forming an angry call of dissent. I pulled myself from groping claws, swung a punch, and managed to kick that nosey Emma onto her back, but the man I had rescued from the Mega-Tree had thrown himself on top of me, still half naked, sending us to the ground. A pair of hands grabbed my ankles. Two more grabbed either arm. I was lifted up and carried away despite my wild convulsions; a paroxysm of indignity. The blurring wall of fiery shadows parted for us, as I was carried and dropped onto my knees, forced to look up at Shepard, smirking as he loomed over me.

You'll see. You'll see, my Witness. This sacrifice will restore order. Your dog will appease the trees... It has to.

Maybe I could have stopped him from doing it if I reasoned with him. Maybe he wouldn't have done it if I swore or insulted him. And maybe he wouldn't have had his skull caved in with my fist if I had begged. But I did nothing. I watched, dismayed, as he held up Diva, who looked to me with pleading, helplessly human eyes, like a child would have, descending into the trench and tossed her over the wall with a callously careless spin.

With this offering, we satisfy you! Return! Return to your harmonious state!

...There was nothing... No tremble of trees shrinking back to size. No thundering voice of God or gods. No angelic call from a being of light emerging from the paddock. Nothing but the hush of the flames. Nothing but the relief of hands pressing down on me easing, stunned by the absence. Nothing but the rush in my ears as I ran down to Shepard, turning to meet me with his disappointed, doleful eyes, before I punched him in the face. Nothing but the slap of a second punch, and then a third, and another, and another. Nothing but the frantic sobs and wails as I sat on top of him, cutting open my knuckles on his face, tenderised, becoming misshapen and warped with each blow, drenched in blood from his broken nose and mangled teeth. Nothing but the guttural gurgle of bubbling spit, blood, and bile in a feeble call for help as his skull began to cave and a bulging eye finally popped out with a satisfying squelch. Nothing but my exhaustive breath mingling with the excruciatingly enduring rhythm of punches, continuing to imprint themselves into Shepard, who went limp. Nothing. That's all we had. That's all we have. Nothing.

I don't know for how long I was still savagely beating Shepard for, nor how long I just sat on top of him, crying for Diva, seeing the black, sappy puddle pooling in his exposed cranium; a choppy stew of brain. But when I was ready I stood up, lifted Shepard, clumsily pushed him up and over the wall, letting it vanish with a roll, and ascend the trench, about to try making my way though the mortified village of onlookers, who had just watched their would-be messiah get decimated by a non-believer.

And then, I heard her.

I froze, we all did, with the first echoes of Diva's barks emanating from the paddock of trees. As though to reward my slow turn back to face them, the trees allowed for another round of barks. I knew there was no proof that was her. For all I knew, this was how the trees were finally going to get me; with the promise of peace. But I didn't care. My Diva needed me. With dutiful commitment, I shuffled back down into the trench, climbed up the wall, and jumped in.

Screadaíl. Thart timpeall. Stoirmiúil. Tá sé le mothú thart timpeall orm. Seasim. Lag. Tuislím. Siúlaim go mall.

Nílim liom féin.

Tá siad go léir anseo. Táimid cruthaithe de phíosaí beaga bána agus dubha. Tá siad go léir cailte.

Breathnaím ar an spéir. Tá cuma an uisce uirthi. Lámh ar mo chos. Is fear gan aghaidh é. Thug mé cic dó. Siúlaim arís.

Ann! Sin í! Mo mhadra! Tugaim barróg di. B'fhiú é.

Is fiú í.

I rolled over the top of the paddock wall, tumbling and landing with a painful smack, cutting myself on the jagged stones and the weedy stalks. We huddled there for a moment, trying our best to recover. Diva, shaking in a slowly calming spasm, tries to nuzzle into me as much as she can, tucking in her paws and ears, burying her whimpering face into my neck. In return, I dug my strained and shaking fingers into her small, frail body. If I was hurting her, I think she resisted a squeal only because the pain meant she was safe.

I kept my promise.

I stood up, marching up the trench, to find the mass of onlookers, the village that was once Leixlip, soon to be a ghost town, still standing there, as a sliver of dawn penetrated the gap outside the Mega-Tree's reach. As we trekked through the large gathering, parting for us as we went, I don't know for how long they were waiting, but, as one of them stepped out from behind us to speak, I soon found out what they were waiting for.

Well... is that it?

I froze, ensnared by the demanding tone, insulted by the insolent ignorance. I turned to face them, wondering how best I could tell them to go fuck themselves, how to even begin to explain the godless void they had submitted to in a single night of indulgent madness, or how to justify to myself the strength it would take to not do to them what I did to Shepard. But I didn't do any of that. After all these months, though I sometimes entertain myself with the question of what it would be like if I did give in to those temptations, I am still glad I approached and snatched the torch out of their hand, crossed back to the paddock, unencumbered by the parting sea of faces, and hurled the torch over the wall, into the trees.

There was the quick dying of light as the flames vanished behind the paddock wall, with the ease of a blown out match. For one quiet second, it was funny, appropriately disappointing. So this is what Shepard must have felt. No wonder he gave up in the end.

But then, in a growing chorus of what sounded like ringing crystal voices from the mouths of heavenly angelic choirs, a hum of light and a high note of an ear titillating crescendo, the clear pastel sky was alive with billions of small glowing orbs in place of the Mega-Tree, disappearing in a blink. In a wave of sublime awe, the heat of the flickering flames was extinguished with dropped torches and candles, falling in the desolated, muddy pitch, leaving a vacuum for the refreshing chill of wonder to flood in and fill. They hung high above us like pulsating miniature stars, aloft and gracefully meandering, unsure if they were to regroup or disperse. Some drifted on the breeze. Others dipped and bobbed, waiting for their turn to rise up into the sky as the topmost orbs were doing. The paddock, once thick and daunting with its fortress of horrors, was growing dull and empty as the heavy curtain of orbs rose higher, free to float and ascend. Away in the distance, far behind where the trees stood, a field, wide and open, was revealing itself, distorted by the refraction of the orbs.

We didn't stay. Not as long as the villagers, anyway. Myself and Diva, who was still snuggling into me for reassurance, walked across the field of villagers, now unmoving in their oblivious trance, forcing us to weave and skirt around them, passed the opening gap between the normal evergreens, now idyllic and pleasant, alongside the monastery with the flowers visibly springing back to life, and out of the park, all as a galaxy of light stretched above, joined by orbs from our estate, all slowly vanishing as they drifted higher, leaving us forever. The dawn grew in intensity; dazzling rays announcing a new day. With our home gone, we had no reason to stay, other than to break into Mary's house and go for an overdue sleep.

Finally, we were going to leave Leixlip.

XXIV.

My body ached the next morning. I don't mean later in the morning. I mean the next morning; we slept for twenty-four hours. The blank, open sky visible through the window was slowly being bleached with the sunrise. Silent, sheer clouds were fading in the distance. Pairs of magpies and starlings glided across the sky as I groaned to sit upright in the bed, fighting against sharp throbs of worn and torn muscles.

It wasn't a dream. I could see the sky. I am in Mary's dusty bed. Diva was beside me, inflating with each peaceful snore. And today we'd finally be leaving forever.

Stepping out of the house we found nothing. No distant hush of the motorway, no crackle of car tires, no bangs of doors, no call of cackling gossip, not even the buzz of flight paths overhead. This was it. It was just us. For the last time here, myself and Diva went for a walk.

We made our way past Riverforest, finding the shops, pharmacies, bookies, and the pub all shuttered and closed. Down into this estate is where we all followed the cat. With Diva safe, it was now evident that whatever was in the trees mustn't affect animals the same way as humans. I don't know if finding Diva helped me escape, or even how we got back out, but from Diva's panting smile and dazzling eyes looking back up at my pensive face, I surmised that maybe animals don't worry about the impermanence of existence as we do. I envy them.

Going on up to Confey Bridge, we watched the commuter train stop at the station, have no one get on or off, and then rumble onwards underneath the bridge. Amazingly, the bridge was undamaged by the crash, proudly standing over the wreckage lying jumbled, half-submerged in the canal. To our right, in the pitch of the GAA club, the other plane the cult members used was parked. And then, off in the distance, the last wispy steam billowed from the Intellex Processing campus. It wouldn't surprise me if inside it now "cleaners" are rushing to destroy whatever secrets they don't want getting out. I don't think they had anything to do with the trees. I think the nature of business has just gotten to a point where we can never say for certain we aren't doing bad things. I'm not naïve enough to say that doesn't apply to all of us, but I'm kind of a bitter pinko, so... you know.

From there, we walked the length of the canal, along the paved footpath. Diva barked at all the ducks and swans serenely sailing past. I was just thankful she read my mind and didn't jump in. I had no plans to be reckless twice in one week. We came out at Louisa Bridge, and, like Confey, the silent roads and uninterrupted bird chirps signalled our further lonesome status. It's very peaceful when all the people are gone. It was beginning to be tempting to stay, what with the promise of finally being left alone.

Of course I wasn't serious, as we walked past the Garda station, left empty and unmanned, down past the entrance of Ryevale, and down into Main Street, passing more closed shops, pubs, and restaurants. I did, however, wonder what made everyone leave, besides the obvious haunting trauma. Maybe it was the natural progression finally easing and fading out? There was a morbid fascination for us to stay. We all wanted to see how it would end. Maybe it was guilt? I can imagine it's sickening to see what you're capable of; how readily you can participate in mob mentality. Whatever about living with supernatural trees, it's nothing compared to living with yourself.

The term "ghost town" is fitting, as the traffic lights change at the empty cross roads, since Leixlip was left like many communities in Ireland; abandoned. Even before the trees, businesses opened and closed within months, traffic would never stop on the way to shop in Liffey Valley, Manor Mills, or Blanchardstown. Before the cult took over, you still had flats and shops paying to an oligarchy of landlords who'd rather have windows cloud with dust than lower rents. They'd rather have nothing than less. The trees seem humane by comparison... but that's not difficult. I will miss Leixlip, but I wish I could forget what happened here. That's why they call it a ghost town; because it haunts you.

We were passing the fire station, about to take the hill back up, when I felt an urge I couldn't resist any longer. It's not the call of the trees. No. It's the call of disbelief. I need to see it again. I need to know I didn't just dream it all. Diva must have felt the same, because she was already trotting up the back entrance to the park, skirting around the shattered glass left on the road from the accidentally thrown molotov. Again we met more traffic lights, continuing on with their circuitry, unaware. There's a real sadness to objects like these, forced to carry on. I know they don't have feelings, but that doesn't mean it's any easier to be a light left on to burn out or a fridge humming forever until the meter runs out. We get to leave, but not everything does. Objects, buildings, memories; they're all trapped wherever we put them.

As we passed the shit farm, it did occur to me that with the water treatment facilities, medical offices, stations, and schools that eventually there would be a need for someone to come check on the village. I can only imagine, as we passed the monastery, on the way to the pitch for the last time, how strange and unnerving it'll all seem, like finding the remnants of a lost city, shrouded in the mystery of why it lies in ruin. Congratulations Leixlip; you've joined the ranks of Pompeii and Pripyat. Not even Lucan can say they have that honour.

Diva waited for me at the gap between the evergreens, still standing silent and uninterested. I joined her and found myself facing the tempting allure of a void. Once again, there was nothing but a field, stretching wide for acres. Without the mass of people standing here the previous morning, the vast expanse only appeared even more desolated. I stood there, looking over the paddock wall, now crumbling and dislodged, resembling the mound of a desecrated burial cairn.

In the distance, a huge harvester came into the field. The massive machine stopped half way across the field, slowing to a halt. The light from the sun flickered and flashed as the compartment door opened and the driver, tiny at this distance, hung out of it, staring back. They must have been able to see me too, because after a pause, an expressionless moment of consideration, they threw their hand up exaggeratedly, waving. In the same manner, bending with the sway of my arm, I waved back animatedly. They got back into the harvester and went back to work. And that was it. Myself and Diva turned around and left. That was the last time we ever went for a walk through St. Catherine's Park.

Coming back out onto Captain's Hill, a Dublin bus came around the bend, leaving Riverforest, heading down the hill for the city. I knew there was another one in half-an-hour. This was it. What was there left to say? It wasn't a bad place before the trees. Maybe that's why we're all leaving. To try again somewhere else.

I threw a rock through the window of a veterinarians and robbed a travelling crate for Diva. We sat down at the bus stop and waited.

It's a strange feeling, when you think about it; the acceptance of the end. Even if you've been through Hell, there's always a level of disbelief, almost longing. As terrible as something can be, it's disconcerting that it can be so domineering, so powerful, yet still be eviscerated in the cold glare of ceaseless time. What hope is there for us if the things that torture us can end too? Eternal damnation is a greater comfort than a life not lived long enough. I remember hearing that the root etymology of the word "nostalgia" is pain of the past. Amending that, I was feeling "Omegalgia"; pain of the end.

"So... this is it?"

I turned to my left and choked on my own gasp as I saw the man in white from the trees sitting beside me. After all this time, though I had completely forgotten about him, I instantly recognised him as quickly as though he was family. He was the same as the night I first saw him, only now what I couldn't tell was a hoody or a cloak was a large, full length, coarse shawl, like a poncho or ruana, wrapped and tucked to shape around his body. Relaxing, leaning back with his arms folded, he turned and smiled at me.

"I must say, I wasn't expecting this. Usually no one leaves, now everyone's gone! Ha! Ah, well. Every time is different, I suppose."

I swallowed what little saliva I could summon from my dry throat and spoke, pointing stupidly, unsure what else to do.

"You're the man I saw that night in the trees."

"That's right. And this must be the delightful Diva. Hellooo! Who's the woo-woo girl! Who's the precious little woo-woo girl!"

The man bent down and slipped a finger in through the grill of the crate's door and, to my surprise, Diva licked it hungrily, as friendly and loving as if it was mine. I watched for a moment, still shocked, like meeting a famous celebrity or world leader; distantly familiar, intimately estranged. In my cloudy state, I blurted out thoughts I had kept to myself this entire time, hoping this was a chance to finally have them answered.

"What... what happened?"

"What do you mean?"

"...What do you mean 'what do you mean'? All of it! Everything that happened! What did it mean? Why did you do all this?"

The man quickly pulled out his finger but was slow to turn to me, trying to compose himself, failing to hide his glower of offense.

"You know what happened. You saw what happened. Why do you think there must be more? Is what happened not enough? Who are you to be lucky enough to be alive, to be able-bodied, to be free, to be thinking, and still ask for more? Who are you to survive this world and demand it comforts you?"

"That's not what I meant. What about the people who are gone? The people I saw go. The people I saw in there! What about them? Do their lives not mean anything?"

"What has meaning to do with what happened to them? And what good would it do for them? Would you be happy if I gave a good enough reason? Is that all it would take for you to applaud what you saw? If I said they died to appease a hungry god, stopping him from devouring the world, would you say you approve? If I said they were all devil-spawn, would you say good riddance? And if I said there was no reason in particular, then and only then you'd feel wronged? Are they as concerned for meaning as you wherever they are? Would they feel cheated if vanishing from this world was just that and nothing more? Would meaning really be a comfort? Has it ever been? Why must life be more than lived?"

I didn't know what to say. I still don't know. I figured I'd carry on, see can I get a direct answer for something else.

"Can I ask you something personal?"

"I'm sure you can."

"What are you?"

"Oh..."

The man chuckled, leaning back, his eyes looking up in amused contemplation, sighing, bowled over by the breadth of the question.

"We've been called different things. Fomorians. Aos Sí. Leprechauns has been the most demeaning so far. I don't know what we are, to tell you the truth. I guess we're like you; just things forced to exist, except we don't worry about it as much as you lot. Ha! I know a joke that explains it pretty well."

"A joke?"

The man giggled.

"Yeah, so, there's two cows in a field, eating grass. The first cow asks 'Why are we here?' The second cow goes 'To eat grass.' The first cow says 'No, I mean what are we doing with our lives? What's our calling? What are we meant to live for? Why are we REALLY here?' And the second cow, without thinking, says 'To REALLY eat grass.'"

The man smiles at me, expecting a reaction. I don't get it.

Our awkward silence doesn't have time to seep upon us for long as the bus appears at the corner, turning slowly. I stood up, taking Diva's crate in my hand. My other hand flew to my pocket as it suddenly dawned on me my phone wallet was still missing. I had only just turned back to the man, about to ask if he could spare money for the fare, when I saw he was holding out my phone wallet. Taking it, I went to speak, as the bus pulled up, but the man answered my question first.

"Does it matter?"

The doors opened. I pulled out my fare card to buy myself some time.

"Well... goodbye."

He just smiled.

"Goodbye, Thomas."

I pulled myself away from all the other unanswerable questions I could spend forever asking. We got on the empty bus, ignoring the shocked stare of the bus driver, sat at the back, and wistfully watch Leixlip pass us by, vanishing from view as we turned the corner after the bridge over the river, whispering under my breath, as Diva settled in to sleep;

"Goodbye."

About the Author

Conor lives in Ireland, studied Film and Animation at Dundalk Institute of Technology and the Irish Film School, and enjoys coffee, doodling, and sleeping in.

Read more at conormatthewswriter.com.